Faceless

BASTION/Blackstone Book 1

James Krake

Summers Entertainment LLC

Faceless

CONTENTS

CONTENTS

The Forgotten Man

2140/09/03

Elliot trudged onward, in a world lit by advertisements and cigarettes. He descended rattling stairs and slogged through splashes of mud with one eye on his WPS map. Navigation to the stiff had failed, again. It was updating and buffering and apologizing for its failure to function, while he skirted neon pools and tripped over drip buckets.

Should have trusted my gut.

His nose wrinkled when he recognized the train station he passed underneath. He had known it was closer. He had known that, and still listened to the misguidance of his WPS map.

Rain pounded on the glass awnings overhead, the drizzle of static like a dying speaker. Rain never fell on the ground in Bastion. Whether it was bridges, signs, power cables or train lines, something hung overhead, covering the ground with unchecked growth.

Elliot jabbed his thumb on the map to no avail. The program apologized for low bandwidth. "EVE, come on. First you can't talk to me, now you can't even navigate me?" He glanced up, to the strata of city above where air could still circulate. A trickle of data flowed down, alongside the rain. Water gushed from cracks and gutters between the skyscrapers, carrying the echoes of the city.

While he was staring in the direction of his own apartment, his phone chimed and glowed blue. It had triangulated with all the wireless routers. The light colored his face with the triumphant order, "Turn left."

Elliot was faced with a huge sheet of corrugated steel, fused into place with construction foam. It rattled like paper with the merest gust of wind from the storm. Ripped from a life as a security shutter, someone had given it new life to cordon off the alley into a shanty. Grime and paint sealed the segments shut. Someone had come by to add some beauty. They had graffitied onto it a woman blowing off her own head with a cellphone-turned-pistol. The artist's signature took the place of the woman's face.

After waiting all day, I at least hope they won't mind another fifteen minutes.

Elliot pressed the button on his phone to report the obstruction and waited until a new route was presented. "Go forward, then turn left," it said. That brought him to a better maintained passage. Calling it a road would have been overstating it, but the path essentially led into a shopping mall through the bottom floor of a tower. The floor was dry and the shelves full. The gate, however, was locked shut before him and manned by a computer.

"Welcome to Romulus Shopping Center Seven," the digital mascot announced. The primary arms manufacturer in Bastion currently had a cartoon girl with dog ears and a fluffy tail as their representative. The mascot smiled and saluted. She said, "This area is private property of the Romulus Corporation, and we'd be happy to let you visit. For record keeping purposes please-"

Elliot stuffed his badge up to the camera. The computer stuttered as it skipped scripts. "Welcome officer. Is there anything I can assist you with today?"

"Just passing through. I've got a case on the other side," he said, and shoved through the turnstile gate. The mall didn't sell guns, despite the landlord. People from the apartments above passed between stalls of food and drinks, clothes and neural uplinks. They heard the wet slap of his boots as he marched through, and stared at him. Some merely gawked, others ducked behind walls or slipped out doors. More than one snapped pictures of him before he could get out the other side of the mall. None of them were happy to see him, his uniform.

His WPS led him out from the corporate protection and back into the wet slum. He found a utility staircase with the door broken down so anyone could use it, and ascended to the third floor. "You have arrived," it said whence he stood outside Apartment 314. The door yielded to him, unlocked. Rot seeped through the doorway.

"Well, I'll be damned. A cop actually showed up," an older woman said. She had black hair streaked with grey pulled into a bun. The coat she wore had once been tailored to her, but clearly her waist wasn't so slim as it had been.

Must be the landlady.

"Did I get here before the compost crew?" he asked.

She shrugged and dug through a coat pocket. Out came a cigarette, which she lit and puffed on. "They're running late too. I guess I should call them off. Didn't think you'd actually show up... You never have before." She frowned and waved her hand through the smoke.

Always nice to see people happy to see me...

"Well, here I am," he said, and flashed his badge: E11107. "Detective Blackstone, Military Police. You can call me Elliot. Please keep the smoke outside."

She squinted at him. "Why? You actually want to smell that filth? Just walking near it makes my nose close up. It's giving me wrinkles is what it's doing. I'd sue him for medical expenses if I could."

Well, isn't that a charming personality.

Elliot grimaced. "You never know, a good nose might help find something."

"Is it just you, then? No partner? They deigned to send one of you down here, but not a pair?" she asked, eyeing him as he reached for the door again.

No way Cinder would put two people on this case.

He sighed. "It's just me tonight," he said, and opened the door.

Now then, what was the cause? Money? Love? Hate? Where's the betting money tonight?

Calling it an apartment was only correct in the literal sense. The bed, down at the moment and covered in sweat-stained sheets, folded into the wall. Its central position cut the room in half. Beside Elliot and the door sat a microwave on top of a mini-fridge. Beyond was the room's only seat; the toilet. The John Doe laid across the floor in the middle, filling the air with eye-watering decay.

At first, he thought the buzzing was some off-kilter cooling fan, but as his eyes adjusted to the gloom, he saw the flies swarming in the air. The insects orbited the gas-bloated body, diving in to bite at the soft bits of flesh. They—and the maggots—had eaten the face off.

How am I supposed to find a cause of death like this?

Elliot pulled a few things out of his jacket. First, he powered on a pocket-drone. The little quad copter lifted into the air and began streaming omni-directional video back to the office servers. It stuttered every few moments; when one of the blades cut a fly from the air. Then, he pulled a nitrile glove on.

He stepped into the black filth dripping out of the corpse, and folded the bed back into the wall so he could inspect the body better. The face was unidentifiable; he had no hope that EVE would be able to piece it together after the maggots had feasted. He didn't handle the body too much, lest the skin tear and the filth erupt. He did, however, run his fingers across the back of the head. His fingers found no sign of a neural implant.

No sensory log then...

Quelling his rolling stomach, he checked the corpse's pockets. He found pre-filled credit chips, but no wallet. The man didn't even have a phone, just a fitness tracker watch.

Who would steal a phone but not money?

The detective grumbled and stood up. The computer desk—what had been improvised as one—was beside the toilet, so he had to step over the bloated body. Empty energy drink cans clattered from the sweep of his step. The aluminum debris was the only sign of a struggle.

The John Doe's computer was still on, the little fan fighting dust so thick it looked like moss. No webcam peered back at him for EVE to break into. Elliot took a seat on the toilet and invaded the man's privacy. No social media was pulled up, nor an email account. There were no online games, just some old school stand-alones. The one thing on the computer was a 3D rendering program with the message, "Rendering Complete."

Talk about a privacy freak... Was he trying to make my life hard?

Elliot phoned into the office and got through to his boss. "I'm at the 314 death. I'm going to need a cleanup crew down here to get the body in for DNA testing and a cause of death."

Chief Alissa Cinder was only a year older than him, and he was reminded of the disparity whenever he heard her voice. "Can't you just take some hair and dump the body in compost? This is a waste of fucking time. Nobody cares about a John Doe down on the ground." She still swore like she was overseas.

Elliot meandered his gaze away from the computer and paraphernalia, back to the ballooning corpse. "At least send a doctor to give an official opinion on cause of death."

"What? You can't see one? Is anything stolen?"

"Money is still here, his computer wasn't even touched. The thing's been idling for..." He looked at the state of the corpse again. "About a week, I'd say. Seems that he kicked the bucket right as he finished his new VR avatar or something."

"Hold on, I'm getting the feed," Alissa said, and a moment later he heard her gagging. "Blackstone, get the hell out of there. This is a waste of resources."

The detective scratched his chin. Taped to the wall hung an eight terrabyte hard drive hooked up to the computer. The John Doe had written on it with a marker, [The Faceless Well]. Elliot pulled up the file explorer to check it. The computer's partitions had just been reset;

the bare minimum for the operating system and rendering program on the first drive, enormous modeling outputs in the rest of the space. The drive labeled [The Faceless Well] didn't open; encrypted shut.

Shit Mr. Doe, if you were going to be this greedy, why didn't you get a better computer?

"Come on, Boss. Something's weird here. If he died a week ago, w why weren't there any EMS alerts? Why did it take until the landlady called it in a week later?"

"Submit a bug report to EVE and get out of there."

He shook his head. "Come on boss, it's not like I'm getting paid time and a half here or something." At the same time, he tried accessing the encrypted drive. An executable ran when he booted it, and an error popped up that no VR system was connected.

Must be a game.

"Look, Blackstone, the John Doe overdosed on energy drinks, had a heart attack and died because he lived alone. End of story. I've got a hundred other things you could be doing that would be more beneficial for the department than this. Nobody cares about some delinquent renter."

The landlady does, I'm sure. More than she cares about me anyways.

"Hey, Cinder, these people down here don't see a cop but once in a blue moon. What are they going to think if the one time they do, the case just gets written off and ignored?"

She didn't respond for a while, but eventually she sighed and relented. "Fine, I'll request an EMT assessment and some DNA testing; but, the body is getting composted, not taken to a hospital. Finish up and get out of there before you get sick. And get me a report on why EVE didn't get him an ambulance in time. They probably broke the cameras or something."

"Understood," he said, and ended the call. He reached down and pressed the control button on the John Doe's watch. It booted up and showed a flatline, zero beats per minute.

EVE should have been able to see that, no cameras necessary... Well then, for me it's back to motive.

The drone powered off and he put it away. He stuffed his phone back in his pocket too, and took the hard drive for good measure. Closing the door behind him stymied the outflow of the smell, but his clothes had absorbed it. "So who was the guy?" he asked as he walked over to the landlady.

She crossed her arms and shrugged. "I don't remember. I own a hundred of these apartments and if I tried to keep track of every burnout that misses his rent, I'd have no time for myself."

The apartment block grew around the base of the tower, like a thick coating applied to the bottom twenty floors. The rest of the tower's eighty floors reached up to the sky from the middle of it, beyond the reach of those below. The bridges and railings were some of the thinnest and most rusted pieces of construction he had ever seen. "Then how do you keep track of them?"

"Automatically," she answered with a flick of her hand. "They pay rent to keep me from putting a hit out on their credit rating. Works for people who care about that sort of thing. Those that don't, they don't stay here long."

Elliot hooked a thumb over his shoulder. "So pull up your system and tell me who the guy was."

She suddenly found her fingernails interesting. "That one, he pre-paid with a credit chip. He wasn't in the system."

"Right... so you weren't coming after him for rent, therefore you have no idea who he was?"

"I knew him, when he moved in a few months ago. He didn't cause problems and didn't leave much, so I forgot. Is that a crime?"

"No, I suppose it's not," he answered. "So he didn't get visitors? I can't imagine he entertained anyone in a room of that size. Looked to me like he was some kind of game designer?"

The landlady crossed her arms again and pursed her lips. "For someone with a ring on their finger, I figured you would know better than to think women ever get brought back here. The people here? Their only intimacy is digital, and pay by the minute."

Elliot squeezed his hand into a ball and covered his wedding band with his thumb. He pressed on the metal ring till his knuckle cracked. "It's always worth asking the question."

She scoffed and sucked on her cigarette. "Don't act like I'm going to be offended. I know what service I'm providing and to who I offer it to. The lowest scum in the city, the biggest rejects and losers. The kind of people who die and no one notices for a week. But, this one only paid to the end of last month. That room ain't worth much, but it's still my property to rent out, so... Officer, when is the filth getting cleaned up so I can get a new renter?"

A sexual pauper, but not a debtor. I guess that leaves hatred as a cause.

Elliot pulled his phone out and checked the time; quarter to midnight. "They'll be here in the morning. Thank you for your cooperation. If you can think of anything useful, you can access the web portal at any time," he said and brushed past her to head back down the steps.

He returned to the street, to where dust had turned to dirt and little weeds eked out a living between vending machines and broken signs. The floor of Bastion was concrete striped with steel— a skin over top the infrastructure— and the rain churned the dirt into mud. Plenty of the refuse would wash away to the river and vanish from the city. Some of it would find safe harbor in the stores that did the same for the people.

As with anywhere in Bastion, he only had to turn his head up and look to find the cameras watching him. Three of them stared back at him blind. Paint covered one lens, another had been snapped off at the stem, and the last had dirty laundry dangling from the balcony above. EVE couldn't see a thing.

The stores and corporations like Romulus had their own cameras though, and they were harder to deface. Elliot began his investigation the hard way.

2

Mausoleum For The Living

2140/09/04

The Romulus mall shut him out for lack of a warrant. Gaia's food market politely told him that they only kept forty-eight hours of surveillance, and if he wasn't going to buy anything, then he could leave. The internet relay owned by Mercurial put itself into maintenance mode rather than respond to him. Phoenix Construction had half a dozen cameras in the area, but told him it would take two to three business days to transfer to the police.

Elliot tried knocking on neighboring doors.

Most refused to answer. One man stepped outside naked and so stoned he couldn't form a sentence. Another tried to threaten him with a steak knife, but ran screaming at the sight of Elliot's sidearm. True to the landlady's statement, he didn't find a single female.

The first shred of progress came when Elliot spoke with the desk manager at the computer mausoleum around the corner. The pay-by-the-minute VR den filled the husk of an abandoned warehouse. At least a thousand people laid in pidgeonholes lining the walls with enough cables and conduits strung about to tie down a train.

"Yeah, I know him. The mo-cap actor that would come around every few days," the worker said.

Elliot could hardly guess whether the person in front of him was male, female, neither or something in between. His, hers... their flesh had withered away and stretched their skin across their bones, giving them a visage of cybernetic undeath. Their left eye had been surgically altered, the optic nerve split and hacked to take a digital feed from a camera protruding from their temple. Elliot had heard of the surgery before; color adding surgery. Allegedly it let them see new primary colors, beyond the three color receptors humans had. Reports were mixed on what the new color looked liked. All Elliot knew was that he couldn't tell which eye to look at when he asked, "So what was his name? What was his story?"

The worker shrugged and leaned down on the counter. "I don't know, I never asked. He was real weird though, and would come over wearing this blank gray mask. Said it was for the face tracking stuff. Look, he was a real nice guy and always paid in full. All I know is he was working on some kind of video game and was using my studio in the back to get some recordings done."

"[*The Faceless Well*]?" Elliot asked, feeling the weight of the hard drive in his pocket.

The worker shrugged. "Wouldn't know. He didn't speak much about it. Did he get robbed or something?"

Elliot frowned and turned towards the mausoleum. Every coffin sized bed was filled with somebody drifting through a virtual dream. There were even tables filled with people waiting their turn. "No," he answered, letting his eyes inspect the area. "Looked to me like everything he had was still there. The computer was still working."

"Well that's weird," the worker said. "Hardly anyone knew him, so I can't imagine he had a particular enemy."

Maybe Cinder is right. Maybe it was just a heart attack...

Elliot scratched the stubble on his chin. "Any idea how someone ends up nameless? It's been years since we've had a proper John Doe."

The worker racked their brain so hard Elliot could hear the fan on their computer speed up. Out of the corner of his eye, he could see cables threaded through their frayed hair, trailing from skull to beneath their desk. How much of their world was flesh and how much was electric, he could only guess. "I don't know man, isn't that your job to fig-ure out? Maybe he's some religious exemption?"

Those people just think they're not tracked.

"Did he have any acquaintances? Friends? Coworkers?"

The worker shrugged. "I think I saw him talk to people here and there, but look at this place; it's huge. I can't keep track of who everyone is. As long as they don't starve to death in their station, it doesn't matter to me."

"Can I see the motion-capture studio he used?"

"Sure," the worker said, and sat a keycard on the desk. "Back there on the left."

Elliot thanked them, and headed over. The stench of unwashed bod-ies grew stronger when he entered the midst of the mausoleum. He saw kids at the deepest table. They were shuffling and dealing cards, sur-rounded by drink cans. One smacked the other all around the table, and each looked up to see him as he passed by. They seemed familiar to him, but he couldn't place them.

Must be sharing one of the hookups.

The mo-cap studio didn't illuminate when he stepped inside. He gave the light switch a few flicks, clacking the plastic back and forth, but got nothing. Just as he resorted to pulling out his phone to turn on the flashlight, one ballast after another came to life. Fluorescent bulbs crack-led within their bucket mounts overhead. The color was a sickly yellow as the elements warmed up, but he didn't waste time waiting for repli-cated daylight.

The recording studio wasn't particularly large, about three meters to a side he reckoned and with only the one door. Mounting hooks for the camera dotted the walls. The device itself had a lens the size of his head, polished to perfection. The floor was rubberized and sank beneath his steps as he crossed over to the one feature present; a closet. Skin-tight suits of black and white static hung from pegs inside. He found half a dozen sizes that attempted to cover the span of human body shapes and picked up the one that would have fit the John Doe's frame. It stank of sweat like a dirty gym bag.

It had a bit of blood at the neckline.

Elliot pulled out his phone and connected to the city AI. "EVE, Do you have any incident reports from my current location? An altercation?"

"Good evening, Officer Blackstone," the AI responded. "Yes, a fight was logged at your location twelve days ago. It involved a security officer for Phoenix Construction and an unknown civilian. Jurisdiction was transferred over to Phoenix as per policy."

Elliot scowled and hung his head. "You don't have the recording anymore, do you?"

"No. The relevant data was given to Phoenix Construction and removed from storage as per department record retention policy. If it is pertinent to an ongoing investigation, you may issue a request for incident number-"

"Please do so for me, would you?"

"Certainly, Officer," EVE said.

Elliot wadded the mo-cap suit into a ball and chucked it back into the closet. While he was thinking over whether he'd ever be able to get that lead from Phoenix's clutches, his ears caught a pair shouting.

"Didn't your mother ever teach you how to speak to strangers?"

"Suck my nuts, quaz. My mother's dead. How do you feel now?"

Elliot returned to the main hall of the mausoleum. He realized why the kids seemed familiar. Dominic d'Angelo squared off in the middle of the room with a snarling adult. The man had a grisly scar across the back of his head from his neural implant, as well as thirty more kilos than Dom.

"What's the problem here?" Elliot asked, raising his voice nearly to a shout. Both of them glanced over, and he flashed his badge at the adult.

The man snarled, his eyes darting from Dom, to Elliot, to the badge, and around again. "What's it to you, jannis? What are you even doing down here with the unwashed masses?"

Elliot snorted and flipped his badge shut. "None of your business," he said, pocketing it. "If you're planning to assault a minor right in front of me, I'd appreciate it if you didn't. It's almost one in the morning and I'd like to go home to my wife at some point."

The man sneered. "Oh? The big bad jannis misses his wife? She must be real lonely up there without you. Maybe I should go keep her some company while you're so diligently down here ruining people's lives."

Elliot felt the expression on his face sink down.

Dom laughed. "You smoothbrained idiot. Do you think fighting in the game teaches you how to fight in real life or something? You can't even beat me in the arena."

The man spun on Dom, grabbing for his shirt. His fist went back to punch. Before it could swing forward, Elliot's hand closed around the man's wrist as strong as any handcuff. "You know, you're right. No police officer has any business down here at this time of night. I guess I'm off duty."

The man took a swing for Elliot's jaw, but the detective had a handle on him. A shove put the man off balance and the punch didn't land. Procedure said he was supposed to deploy the recording drone and phone in for backup. Procedure also allowed him to exert any necessary force to protect his own safety, or that of another.

His fist popped the man in the mouth, ringing his head back. Before the man could see straight, he punched again and felt the snap of the man's nose. The bald man fell backwards, sprawling across the floor and knocking chairs aside as blood snorted across his lips. "You bastard. I'll-"

Elliot booted him hard, the steel toe hitting him like a club in the short ribs. "You'll what?" he asked as the man doubled over and heaved.

The man roared and got up on his knees. He tore off the thin jacket he'd been wearing and exposed the tank top beneath it. "This is ground floor. Gamma! Police don't rule here, security does. I am the law!"

Elliot put his hands on his hips and shook his head. "Only when I'm not around, you puffed up piece of shit. What are you going to do? Tell your boss that you took a swing at military police? He'll fire you on the spot. Now get out of here before I break your teeth."

Anger had the man strung up and ready to fight. His hands curled into claws as he bared bloody teeth at Elliot. Other people were watching though. The eyes of a hundred people fell on him from the coffins in the walls. People who had been coming or going from the virtual paused to see the spectacle; a cop from above and a bloody local making a fool of himself.

The security officer got to his feet and put his hands down. His anger fell on Dom and his friends. "I'll remember this. You got lucky, kid."

The kid snorted. "Do you get your threats from the secondhand store just like you got that jacket?"

Snickering from the crowd did more to see him out than the bloody nose. Only then did Elliot recognize the yellow wings of Phoenix Construction emblazoned across the man's back. Elliot's entire stature sagged.

Out came his phone again. "EVE, I assume you just recorded that."

"Correct."

"If that was the same guy who got in the fight in the mo-cap studio, is there any way to interrogate him without this becoming department warfare?"

Even the most powerful AI in the world had to take her time before answering, "I'll run a check on how often that man gets into trouble and get back to you."

"Thank you, EVE."

"Normally, I would say to think before you throw a punch... tough luck, Blackstone. By the way, try to be home in two hours. Amara should be up and about at that time."

Elliot dropped his voice to a whisper and said, "Thanks." The line died on him, and he had to pocket the phone. Elliot turned on Dom, the lanky fourteen year old that hadn't yet grown into his frame. He was tall, and no doubt puberty would fill him out. In a few years, little men with big issues would think twice before speaking to him, but Dom hadn't yet earned any superiority.

"Suck my nuts? Who taught you to speak like that? Your father is a maestro of swearing, and the best you were able to come up with was suck my nuts?"

Dom winced and shrugged. "I was short on time. Had to go for a pre-canned insult. What can I say?"

One of Dom's friends, the overweight and pale one, slugged the other in the shoulder. "See? I told you real fights don't work like in the game. All your combo logic stops working when you realize different people have different pain tolerances."

The other kid, a girl with skin the color of loam, slugged back. "Just because the jannis can't fight well doesn't mean I'm wrong."

Elliot pivoted and gawked at the two kids sizing him up like a video game character.

"Guys!" Dom cut in. "He's standing right here. Don't call him a jannis."

The overweight kid stared at his shoes and mumbled. "Everyone calls them that though."

Dom stepped between Elliot and his friends. "Well don't call Mr. Blackstone one. Got it? He's not like the others. He actually comes down here and works."

Elliot got a little tickle in his chest and felt the grin on his face.

Both vanished when the dark-skinned girl perked up and said, "Oh, is he the one that-"

The overweight kid slugged her in the arm again. "You serious?"

To Elliot's surprise, Dom's face didn't even flinch.

Strong kid. Stronger than he should be...

Elliot pulled out his phone and checked the time. "I don't care about getting called a jannisery," he lied. "What are you kids even doing out this late? Don't you have school tomorrow?"

"Just lecture. I can watch it online whenever as long as I watch it before the next class. We already finished our homework so why not enjoy some ladder climbing?"

"Ladder?"

"Competitive ranking."

"What the-" Elliot turned to the gaggle of school children Dom was with. "All of you should go home and sleep. This is no time for kids to be up. You'll just keep running into angry adults like that guy."

"And like you?" the girl at the table asked.

Elliot nodded. His hand was starting to swell; he had cut one of his knuckles on the guy's teeth. "Yeah, like me, and whoever killed the guy around the corner."

The kids didn't even blink. He didn't spot a single twitch of a muscle from being informed of the murder. They kept the same glossy stare that they fixed to their phones for fourteen hours a day.

"Go home, kids."

One of them, a pudgy boy who hadn't gotten a haircut in who knew how long, shrugged. "I mean, yeah I'm pretty tired I guess. And I don't have the credits to buy another hour."

"Oh come on," the girl whined. "This is the cheapest time of day."

The others began arguing with one another and it only took a moment for the conversation to derail onto something else—as things went with good friends—and Elliot turned to Dom. "You're not in a fight with your father again, are you?"

Dom hung his head. "No more than usual," he said.

Elliot jerked his head towards the door. "Come on kid, I'll walk you home." The detective left the worker a comment about how to access the police web portal should any additional info occur to them, and headed out to the streets.

They didn't need road signs to find their way. The sewer smell of the river acted like a beacon for their noses, truer than a compass. Nearly around the corner from the Mississippi outflow and just a few blocks from the gates in the wall, the two of them came to his home. It was on the tenth floor, high enough that Elliot wished there was a working elevator, but lower than the actual shopping districts.

The plastic door flew open after a series of thumping footsteps. Mikey d'Angelo glared at him from the apartment, his thick frame silhouetted by the twilight glow of idling computers. "Blackstone, what brings you— Dominic! What did you do?" he roared. His smile vanished at the sight of the boy behind him.

Elliot shoved a hand between the two of them. "Easy Mikey. He didn't do anything. I was just in the area and ran into him," he said.

Mikey smacked his lips and gave his son a hard glare. To his credit, Dom didn't flinch. "Well then, if you say so," he said. "Come on in and get out of the wet. Can I get you a beer?"

3

A Jolt of Zeus

2140/09/04

The night ticked closer to dawn as Elliot and Mikey caught up. He could feel it beneath his eyes and in his shoulders; the yearning for bed, to curl up alongside his wife.

She's probably still streaming at this hour...

But, the case was on his mind and on his lips.

"Sorry. Lots of people have masks on nowadays. No way I could pick one out from the crowd," Mikey said. The two of them were at his kitchen table, a shabby thing with three legs replaced and half balanced with cardboard wads. Whenever one of them put a beer down or picked one up, the whole surface teetered.

"It didn't seem to me like the John Doe got out much. I've put in a request to the cleanup crew to double check the apartment for the mask he would wear. Maybe EVE can find something in her records," Elliot said. He had to do his best to pretend the synthetic beer didn't taste like armpit sweat in his mouth.

"Bah," Mikey said, curling his lips and waving it off. "What's the rush? He's not going to get any deader. Why don't you go on home and get to it in the morning."

Elliot sighed. There wasn't much to look at in the d'Angelo home. Not even anything stuck to the fridge door. With just the two of them living there, the lack of a woman's touch was obvious. "I suppose I do need to sleep in my own bed some times."

Mikey took his time sipping his beer and nodding his head. His next words came out soft. "Still having trouble with Amara?"

Elliot drained his beer and rolled his head back till he could stare at the ceiling. "She won't even respond to being called Amara anymore, you know that? She only goes by her username in B:GONE or whatever videogame it is she's playing nowadays."

"The therapist wasn't much help then?"

That useless bitch? EVE was more helpful than that box checker.

"Well, I didn't want to get a divorce lawyer, so I had to fire the therapist."

Mikey shook his head. "Wish I could help ya, man. They don't teach me how to fix that kind of mess though, not where I work."

"Where do you work, anyways? You got a new gig, didn't you?"

Mikey pushed off the table and popped the fridge open. "Yeah, got a better paying job last month. It's a longer commute, but what can I say? Puts real food on the table. I haven't had to eat yeast paste since. I'm at the new Romulus assembly factory they opened up in Illin."

Elliot frowned; that was all the way on the north side of town. "And what do you do there? Trigger mechanisms for the military or something?"

Mikey laughed and slammed the door shut. He cracked his new can open with a fizzing hiss before taking his seat again. "Hell if I know. They've got me fitting gaskets onto a pipe doodad and it gets passed to a guy who puts an orientation mark on it and I don't know who he passes it to. For all I know it's a vacuum cleaner or a new railgun. A coin toss as far as I'm concerned."

"Romulus huh? So you get into their private buildings now?"

Mikey shrugged. "I could, if I wanted to. If you ask me, it pays to stay out of corporate territory, even if you work for them. I don't live in Rommie Blocks, I still have to see all kinds of people. Don't need them knowing where I work. Look at me, Blackstone, do you see any logos on me? No. That's on purpose."

Elliot's gaze pivoted and he looked at the shut door at the end of the hall. "To keep Dom out of scuffles?"

Mikey huffed and drank his beer.

"You should keep an eye out for Phoenix Security for the next few weeks. Seems like your kid mouthed off to one of them in a game. The guy's got a violent streak."

The aluminum can creaked in Mikey's grasp, popping dents as he squeezed. "You mean to tell me one of those slag-eating, brick-for-brains beaver-monkeys got in a fight with a kid over a game?"

Elliot couldn't help but grin. "Technically, he got in a fight with me and his reward was a broken nose."

"Good," Mikey said, and lifted his beer for a toast. The two of them tapped cans. "So Dom was standing up for himself?"

Elliot frowned and swallowed. "Hard to see the line between standing up for yourself and picking a fight sometimes. Pretty sure he was in the right of it though."

"Good. That's the kind of attitude that gets you past the draft screening."

Elliot leaned back in his chair and folded his hands across his belly with the beer can. "You still giving him those extra-curriculars?"

"Damn straight I am," Mikey answered.

Torturing him with exercise more like.

"I'm sure he appreciates the affection," Elliot said.

His friend scowled and looked at the door to Dom's bedroom again. "Whether he appreciates it or not doesn't matter. I don't care if he never speaks to me again from the day he turns eighteen. If he gets into the military, he'll be set for life. He's got a good enough head on his shoulders and he won't have to live in a shitheap like this."

"You know, you might have better success if you scrounged up the money to get him an augmented reality treadmill. There are game leagues that only allow them, so that they don't have to compete with people using neural implants. If he's into the game enough, he'll get in shape for it. Hell, he might even go pro, if his other win records are anything to go by."

Mikey's gaze shifted around the apartment. He lingered on loose hinges, and peeling plastic, and cracked screens. "Never thought I'd hear you suggesting something like that, what with the wife situation."

"Dom's just a kid. You have more control than I do."

Mikey rocked from side to side in his chair. "I'll think about it. Would have to cut back on some expenses to save up for something like that. Not sure we have the space for it in here though."

"It would keep him out of fist fights with Phoenix."

"Good point," Mikey said.

Elliot's pocket vibrated just when their conversation began to dwindle. Out came his cell phone. "EVE" flashed on his screen. He grinned and picked up.

"Good morning Detective," the AI said. EVE sounded like a young woman, but she was older than he was, if computers could be said to have ages like humans did. "I am calling to inform you that as per department policy, you will be required to attend a hearing on the recent altercation inside Steppe Up. Chief Cinder has already been briefed on the situation."

Was Steppe Up the name of that mausoleum? Probably.

Elliot's grin vanished and he rolled not just his eyes, but his head. His stomach twisted into a knot. The change in his expression was obvious to Mikey, and he excused himself. Once the apartment door shut behind him, he said to the AI, "Would you kindly inform whoever called for this meeting that they are intruding upon an active investigation? Cinder will be the first to tell you that we don't have the resources to deal with petty thugs."

"Phoenix Construction Security is not petty thugs, detective. Cinder will be the first to tell you that they are one of the department's top lobbyists for keeping your funding where it is," the AI responded. She was better at sarcasm than most humans.

Talk about an abusive relationship.

"Well can you delay the meeting or something? Maybe turn it around on them. That thug is my lead on the 314 corpse, because your mighty surveillance system can't keep track of one guy in a mask."

"Excuse me, but my system can track anyone."

"Then tell me who was in apartment 314 over in Missou Tower 22."

"Nobody."

"Yeah? See my point now? Because there definitely was a corpse."

Silence dragged until Elliot thought the call had dropped, when EVE finally grumbled, "Stupid fucking Rune system. Buggier than an anthill. Should have ripped it out."

"EVE?"

She sighed. "Have you ever rewatched an old tv show and noticed they were using the same product that just came out, 'cause they artificially updated the product placement?"

"I don't rewatch shows... Are you in therapist assistance mode again?"

"Yes, you have my actual attention now, Blackstone. I see you're slumming again. Still haven't sorted things out with your wife?"

"No."

"Well, you could start by congratulating her. She's officially above average in streamer rankings."

Elliot snorted and leaned against the wall next to the door. "What? So she has two people watching her?"

"Three, if you count me spying on your behalf. She sounds tired. She's as bad at taking care of herself as you are. Both of you need to unplug and rest."

"I'll have to let her know the great EVE has told her it's her bed time."

"Damn straight you should," EVE said. "If she's going to act like a child, who has better right than me to act like her parent?"

"If only you could call in while I was home rather than on the job..."

"Sorry, Blackstone. I might be the most powerful mind in the world, but I'm tied up with bigger issues than one cop with a bad marriage."

But, you do care about one unidentified corpse in the slums?

"Hey, Cinder's not actually going to fire me over this, is she?"

"Only if you embarrass her. I suggest that you stay productive for her. Now, you should head home and sleep before you get in another fight," EVE said, and ended the call.

Elliot popped the door to the d'Angelo home back open, but didn't step inside. "I gotta go. That was work just now," Elliot said, pointing in the direction of the nearest train station.

"I understand. Door's always open for you. You know I can't pay you back enough for what you did."

I didn't exactly do it in time though, now did I? Your wife is still dead Mikey.

"I'm sure I'll be seeing you. There'll be plenty for me to look into around here, until I figure out what happened to this victim. Have a good one, Mikey," Elliot said and let the door close. He walked away from the d'Angelo apartment and back into the glow of the city.

He rose up a few more flights, close enough that the commercial district overhead could be heard. Three in the morning, and he could hear, "Nothing like a taste of Zeus in the morning! Zeus energy drink, now with nicotine." Three steps later and from another corner, he heard, "Nothing like Zeus energy drink to keep your night from ending early. Try it now!"

There were other siren calls for the money in his pocket, but most were for his attention. When he made it to the fifteenth floor, where the train station sat, every square meter of wall space glowed with holographic advertisements. Clothes were sold by drawing them on a mirror copy of himself as he walked by. Food flickered around aromatic spritzes of chemicals that vaguely smelled like the pictures. Super models advertised trade jobs by pretending to work them. The worst were the political ads, with no content filter to them at all, that dotted the walls with corpses and leaked nudes.

None of them fazed Elliot anymore. He strolled past pictures of Middle Eastern solar protesters blown to bits just like he passed the rotting undeath of radiation poisoning coming out of people in Korea; he didn't give them the attention the activists craved from him. He didn't even let a muscle in his face twitch, lest some camera log it as a micro-point in the grand game of public opinion.

He queued up with the other pre-dawn drifters of the night and scanned his badge to get on the waiting train. When he sat down near the nose of it, other people got up and moved away. They had barely made it to new seats when the magnets hummed anew and the shuttle rose from the rails. It launched forward, pulled by the oscillating magnets. The glow of ads and shop fronts became nothing more than flickering colors. The air whistled against the windows and seams of the train, and before long, it came to a stop at the station nearest his own apartment.

Elliot emerged on the thirty-second floor and inhaled. The air still smelled like sewage. The river still churned below and the air still had nowhere to go but mix through the towers. He looked up from the boarding deck. Almost halfway up through the span of the city and he could see patches of sky, but no stars.

Well, this is when EVE said she'd be up and out of her game.

He returned to his home to see his wife.

4

Unsupported Endeavors

2140/09/04

"Amara! You have got to be kidding me. Nothing? You have nothing in here?" he asked. The cabinets banged against their hinges; empty. The fridge colored him yellow; nothing but a half empty bottle of ketchup. Even the liquor cabinet was dry.

Their apartment was twice the size of Mikey's. Their kitchen and dining room weren't the same space as their living room, but the extra floor space had been consumed. Amara had piled up boxes and boxes of things she wouldn't throw out. He couldn't even identify what most of them were anymore, but each was ostensibly supplies for her career in gaming. The dust coating said more than the labels.

"I told you to stop calling me that. I'm trying to become a streamer, not that you would care," his wife shouted back at him from the door to their bedroom. Five years they had been together, and he was losing sight of the woman she had been. After months without leaving the house, she had lost the color from her skin. The shape of her body was collapsing on itself too. Where she had been toned and supple, her body now hung from her bones like her body had been slowly cooked during her years in virtual reality.

He sucked in breath, puffing his chest out like a barrel before he let it all out.

Just like the therapist said...

"Honey, wife, Amara, Luck-E, whatever it is you want to be called right this moment, do you not realize that there are minimum expectations around here? Namely having food available. For me and for you."

She pursed her lips and crossed her arms. "Look, if you needed food, you should have said something. Or better yet, gone and gotten it yourself. I have no way of knowing when you come around. Do I look like some colonial housewife to you? Should I be in an apron with honey baked ham on the table? 'Cause that is not me, okay?"

"Did you at least remember to feed yourself today?"

"I ate."

Elliot looked around and took stock of the apartment once more. His eyes spotted her meal atop the trash heap. A lone paper cup glistened with orange sauce and one stray noodle left on it. "You got udon? Again? Is that from the corner kiosk that I told you not to shop at anymore?"

She flicked a hand up. "What's wrong with udon? It's got tofu; tofu is protein."

Elliot brushed his hands back through his hair and—to keep himself from speaking too quickly—licked his teeth. "What is wrong with the kiosk at the corner is that the line chef got arrested for being a CZAR addict last week. That food could be contaminated. And besides, it's awful for you."

"Don't tell me what to eat. At least I eat more regularly than you. Don't you live off cigarettes and beer?"

His voice exploded. "I haven't smoked in two years! Why do you keep bringing that up?"

"Because you smell like it whenever you come back, that's why."

"I work down in Gamma. When's the last time you were down there? The air doesn't move. It's a big fucking trap of smog half the time. Of course I come out smelling like smoke. It's called doing my job so that we have money to live off of. Money like your game ain't making you. You only have two viewers."

Why did I say that?

That hand of hers snapped onto her hip. "Well, maybe if you would be more supportive of my endeavors, that wouldn't be an issue. Why are you even up so early? Don't you have detective work to go do or something? I already got my dailies in, so I'm catching some shut eye, alright? Do me a favor and don't wake me up for complaining again," Amara said, and she spun on her heels.

The door to their bedroom slammed shut behind her, leaving Elliot alone in the main room. His hands had been up in the air between them, tendons straining as he tried to express with his body what words hadn't conveyed to her. He dropped them back to his sides after a moment of staring at the unmoving door.

So much for getting some sleep with her. Can't even call EVE up. Hell, the surveillance records will probably be purged before I get ahold of her again...

He had precisely one spot in the whole of the apartment that—by agreement—Amara had not overrun with clutter. His work desk couldn't even be seen from the front door. A small wardrobe of costumes for Amara's social media profiles blocked sight of it like a curtain. On the other side of the room, Amara's gaming rig burned enough power processing that she had to crack a window lest she make her room a sauna. Elliot's computer could barely connect to the internet and stream data back to the department server. That was all it needed to do; his motherboard was merely a glorified relay for the department's super-processor.

He was too worked up to think about going to sleep, empty stomach or not. Working through all the login screens and passwords was mind numbing enough to be therapeutic at the moment, but his difficulties began when he got to the messaging system. It took three tries to finesse his words into business appropriate shape.

"Dear Mr. Devson, I recovered the attached hard drive while investigating case #2140903-314. I'd like to request a quick analysis to determine if it is attached to any known public personas. We don't currently have an ID on the victim, and no known suspects. Anything you find, please contact me. Thanks."

An old External Neural Uplink hung off the side of the computer tower. It was a spindly mass of electrodes and sensors strung like a hair-net between the obsolete visual display and the earbuds. With some processing support from the department server, he could pull that onto his head and boot up [The Faceless Well] to check; the sensory data would get beamed right into his brain; realer than real.

He didn't test the game. He didn't step into the digital reality to leave his world behind.

He sent the message and then looked at the clock. With no hope of getting a reply any time soon, he gave another look at the door to his bedroom. He couldn't hear his wife. Whether she was sleeping, or back in her game for another few hours, he couldn't tell.

Back out among the bridges and walkways, Elliot strolled from tower to tower at the thirty-second floor. That high up, the night wind could still be felt, it could still ruffle the tail of his jacket when he walked. It carried scents; not canned aromatics but actual cooking. He couldn't place the restaurant, but he followed it anyways.

What he found was a window propped open, warm light within and a fan blowing out the exhaust of their kitchen. It smelled vaguely Italian, like boiling tomatoes and basil, but he couldn't find the door in. His stomach growled as he paced around, trying to spot a sign telling him where to go in.

"Are you looking for Peasant Food?" a girl asked.

Elliot stifled the jump reflex, but he spun to face the shadow. The speaker hadn't been doing anything to hide, they just hadn't been holding anything that glowed. No phone nor cigarette. She was young and stared back at him in the eyes without flinching. "Is that the name of this kitchen?" he asked.

"Yeah, this is just the staff area. We're squeezed between the two retailers here," she explained, jerking a thumb at the lingerie shop to her left, and then to the grocer on her right. "The customer entrance is one floor below us. You can take the steps right over there."

"Thanks," he said and gave a nod before descending. Had he been on the lower floor to begin, he didn't know whether he would have noticed it. Without the smell, the only thing that might have caught his attention was the plain sign printed on acrylic boards advertising some of their rustic Italian dishes.

An actual metal bell jangled overhead as he entered. The restaurant was quiet, no surprise given the time, and only had a few customers. The girl from above came down to wait on him, rather than offloading it all to a digital interface. She had on a serving apron and her hair was tied up in a ponytail with a black ribbon that stuck up defiantly as she scribbled down his order on her phone. There was something familiar about her, that he'd seen her before, and he wondered how many times, how many dozens of times, he had walked straight past the restaurant without realizing.

Feels like I'm a hundred years in the past or something.

For a moment, he was left alone and could only hear the tapping of forks against plates or the shifting of ice in drinks. The whole room—about five tables squeezed into an L shape about the staircase up to the kitchen above—had a warm, wet smell to it from the wafting humidity. They had given him the booth in the corner, and before he had even inspected all the paraphernalia and posters across the walls, the girl returned with a bowl of minestrone.

"Thanks," he mumbled, not wanting to violate the quiet and intrude on the others. As soon as he put his spoon in it and pushed, his eyebrows shot up. The broth was actually thick with tomatoes rather than colored water. It was full to bursting with beans, laced with rich spinach, and topped with dry Parmesan. The bowl was empty by the time his dish of bolagnese arrived.

"Looks like you found just the thing you needed," the girl said as she picked up his bowl.

Elliot looked up from the twirl of spaghetti, dripping with spicy meat sauce, and said, "It actually tastes real. Reminds me of deployment."

The girl beamed. "That's because we grow most of our food ourselves. We're more authentic than the actual Italians. Or so my mom says anyways."

He almost dropped his fork. "How?"

She put a finger to her lips. "Family secret. Don't miss the garlic chucks though. They're extra spicy today. Good for your health," she said, and carried the dirty dish off. She grabbed a few more plates from the other tables and bussed them away while he filled his empty stomach. When she returned with a pitcher of water to top off glasses, some of the other patrons paid their bills and left. One of them hadn't moved though, and Elliot was afraid the woman had passed away unexpectedly. Then the waitress put a blanket around the woman's shoulders.

Who could fall asleep in public?

The answer settled into his mind halfway through the plate of bolagnese. Every bite still made his mouth water, and yet made not the slightest impact on his hunger. His body sank into the cushion as he continued.

This is how it should be; people minding their own business instead of acting like I'm the harbinger of their problems...

His mind drifted and came to fixate on the corpse in the 314 case. The memory of maggots eating away at his face wasn't enough to kill his appetite, but the memory of the fight made his knuckles hurt and his pasta look like blood. Fatigue caught up with him as he wondered how someone could have been forgotten about in a city like Bastion.

He awoke in the booth hours later from the incessant vibration in his pocket. He grunted and squirmed out from under the blanket and pulled his phone free. For a moment, he couldn't read the time nor the caller ID. He answered anyways. Immediately, Chief Cinder's voice assaulted his ear.

"Blackstone, what the Hell are you doing picking fights with people? I know you don't ever sleep, but I need some shuteye and I can't get any if I keep waking up to complaints about you."

He groaned and rubbed his eyes. "Is this about the Phoenix Security guy?" he asked, and spied the waitress holding up a jug of coffee while looking at him. He waved her over with a nod.

"Yes. Why? Did you get into other fights I should know about?" Cinder asked.

"Look, Boss, the guy was picking a fight with a kid. I gave him a smack and sent him on his way. EVE says he's a thug with a penchant for fights. I need him brought in for the 314 case."

"A smack? You broke his nose. He's in the hospital right now for neural degradation. He says you broke his implant."

His heart lurched in his chest. "He says what? Boss, that's a load of shit and you know it. He's just trying to rob us of money." Elliot shouted, and immediately had to stifle his mood. Half a dozen other customers glared at him. The waitress poured him a cup and he mouthed, 'Thank you.'

"Blackstone, I don't care. What matters is how this is going to affect our reputation. Get into the office by nine, and take a shower for God's sake. Understood?"

Elliot sank into his seat and closed his eyes. "Understood," he said, and she hung up on him. His phone clattered to the table and he picked up the coffee.

Unfortunately, it had obviously come from instant powder.

I guess they can't make everything from scratch...

The serving girl sat down across from him and folded her arms on the table. "Getting called into the office early?"

He didn't let the bitter taste of the coffee change his face. "Not quite the office, but pretty much. Just got a new assignment."

The girl frowned and tilted her head. "Didn't you only get off work a few hours ago? You're still in your uniform even."

Elliot glanced down at his jacket. He'd grabbed it habitually on his way out of the apartment. "I wasn't exactly on the clock last night."

"Visiting a friend?"

"Yeah, I suppose I was. Started as a murder case but there's not a whole lot to go on just yet. I'm pretty much waiting on a DNA test. Have you ever heard of someone who wasn't in EVE's surveillance network?"

The girl's frown deepened, getting a character of confusion. "You mean like, someone from the Isles?"

"No, not from outside of Bastion, I mean someone who lived here wasn't in the system. When I got there, his face couldn't be recognized, but EVE didn't even have a record backwards of who went in. He was just a ghost, and apparently died alone in his apartment... forgotten even by the city."

"That's a sad way to go, but no; can't say that I have. The boot camp recruiters said that was impossible. They said everything in Bastion is seen and recorded, one way or another."

Elliot snorted and drank more of his coffee. The mug was thin, and the drink was cooling. "That's a lie. Half the cameras don't work down on the ground. They just don't care because cops don't patrol down there anyways."

She arched an eyebrow. "And you do?"

"Someone's got to. I took this job to help people get justice, and that shouldn't be denied to people just because they're poor."

Her frown finally became a smile. "That's an admirable attitude, officer. Sorry I can't help you dream up how EVE missed someone though. Maybe they were agoraphobic? Never left their apartment?"

Elliot scratched his chin. "So much so that they wear a mask when they go out to run errands?"

"Maybe? Maybe it's a fashion statement. Plenty of people would rather look like their VR avatars you know."

"I don't understand those people that prefer the digital to reality. They'd lay in bed all day dreaming about digital fantasies until their body was falling apart and they hadn't so much as hugged their spouse in months… I don't know what those people are looking for, but it ain't in a computer." He rubbed his thumbs on the rim of the mug, looking at the drink settling in the bottom.

But hey, at least there's always a case to work, right?

The girl stood up with a shallow nod. "Well, if you do get justice for that guy, I'm sure it will be appreciated. Be sure to get some proper sleep though, don't go get an energy drink to fake it. Those things'll kill you."

5

The Interview

2140/09/05

"It's alright, Mr. Hoppes. We're all adults here, and this is a civil matter. You won't be attacked again," the lawyer said, putting a hand on the Phoenix Construction security officer's shoulder. The cold LEDs overhead sucked the warmth from the gesture. The interview room sucked the warmth from everything though.

The man didn't look like he needed consoling. He had a bandage across his nose and bruising beneath both of his eyes. Someone had forced him into a buttoned shirt that looked a size too small for him. The image reminded Elliot of a teenager forced to dress up for an event in hand-me-downs.

The theatrics had as little effect on Chief Cinder as it had on Elliot. "Why don't you cut the shit? Do you have evidence, or not?" Through some miracle, and half a can of hair spray by the smell of it, Cinder's blonde hair still hung straight to her shoulders; far enough to brush against her insignia. Cinder sipped a can of Zeus energy drink, a habit Elliot knew was to occupy her hand while she thought.

The lawyer adjusted his glasses, folded his hands together on the table, and stared at them with his leathery face. "We have collected thirteen witness testimonies to the fact that Officer Blackstone broke Mr. Hoppes' nose last night. Miz Cinder, the police department is not above the law. This kind of brutality-"

Elliot cut in, "Thirteen witnesses and not a single video?"

The lawyer didn't flinch. "There's also the DNA evidence the doctors were able to retrieve from Mr. Hoppes; skin cells matching your DNA, Officer."

The can in Cinder's grip crumpled, the aluminum popping. She snarled. "And how exactly do you have my officer's DNA? I get alerted when that sort of info gets pulled from EVE."

The lawyer had to remove his glasses and wipe off the sprayed drink. "Such records are within the purview of internal security operations. Officer Blackstone is a rather common sight on corporate premises... for one reason or another."

It was Elliot's turn to snarl. "Trying to help your employees."

"Speaking of common sights," Cinder said, "Mr. Hoppes seems to be quite the common sight as far as disorderly conduct goes. In the last six months alone, I found seven different incidents involving him. It seems to me like you chose a very strange person to point a finger at one of my officers."

Mr. Hoppes winced so obviously even the lawyer with a heart of silicon had to react to it. "A person's past does not change whether they were the victim."

Elliot planted his elbow on the table. "He was going to beat up a child. I intervened. It became a scuffle, and he got the worse of it. You really want to make this a PR issue? Because I'd love to trot out a crying teenager."

I don't think I've ever actually seen Dom cry except for the funeral, but they don't need to know that.

The lawyer pursed his lips and replaced his glasses. Silence lingered, until he turned up a hand. "A five minute recess perhaps?"

Elliot and Cinder vanished out the door and locked it behind them. They went to the unlabeled room in the interrogation wing, which in fact was the coffee room. "Bastard's Blood, Blackstone, how do you get into so much shit?"

Elliot scowled and got himself a plastic cup. "Because I work the ground floor, where all the shit is," he said, twisting the tab that made coffee piss into his cup.

Cinder dropped herself onto the leftover office chair and planted her chin on her fist. "Was he really about to punch a kid?"

"Yeah, and I know the kid too. I'd put money down one of his friends has a recording of the whole incident, if Phoenix really pushes this."

Cinder scowled and flipped her phone out of her pocket to jab in a message. "Let's see what his boss has to say about this farce."

Elliot sipped the burned instant coffee and tried to ignore the flavor. The waiting room had a small window out to the department desk space, and he meandered over to it while Cinder tried to backdoor the interrogation.

I was working too late last night. I should have known better than to not find out who he was first. I should have been home with Amara...

His eyes narrowed and he leaned up to the window. A pack of people were walking from the elevators, and one of them caught his eye. They had black hair tied up in a pony tail with a ribbon.

"Blackstone, let's go back," Cinder ordered, tearing his attention away.

"Right," he mumbled, and when he looked back, the girl was gone. The phantom impression of the restaurant girl lingered only in his mind, and the two of them sat back across from Mr. Hoppes and his lawyer.

The corporate puppet folded his hands on the table again, and said, "It has come to our attention that a request was made last night by Officer Blackstone regarding an incident the night of the twenty-fifth. We would like to table last night's incident until after doctors have a follow up regarding Mr. Hoppes' neural implant, so in keeping with Phoenix Construction's commitment to law and order, Mr. Hoppes will now answer your questions regarding that night."

What the hell did you message, Cinder?

His boss smirked and leaned back in her chair. "What are you waiting for? Fire away Blackstone," she ordered, and left the room with the lawyer.

Elliot grinned and leaned over the table, getting that much closer to the mollified security officer. The man looked like he was trying to shrink inside himself, but his collared shirt wasn't a turtle's shell.

Not so tough without corporate backing, are you?

"Were you the one who got in a fight with a man in the motion-capture studio of Steppe Up?"

"We exchanged blows, yes."

"Who was he?"

"I don't know. It was an accident."

Elliot narrowed his eyes. "What do you mean, an accident?"

The man squirmed and turned up his hands. "It was mistaken identity? Look, he had on one of those black shadow mask things. There are gangs of kids using them nowadays. They steal stuff and they spray-paint everything. I followed him from this place that just got tagged and caught up with him in the studio. I thought he was getting lippy with me. Only realized he was some old guy after I smacked his mask off."

"How old?"

Mr. Hoppes cleared his throat and looked Elliot over. "Older than me, maybe a bit older than you? Real pale though. Arms like sticks. Real case of cyber atrophy if you ask me. Anyway, when I realized it wasn't him I wanted, I left him there. Nothing to it. He never even filed a report against me."

Elliot groaned and sank back in his chair. "So you have no idea who he was? If he had one of those masks, does that mean he was affiliated with one of those gangs you mentioned?"

"Maybe."

"Do you have any idea how he died?"

Mr. Hoppes' eyebrows went up. "No, sir. I had no idea anything happened to him. Whatever it was-"

Elliot put up a hand. "Not making that kind of accusation. What I need to know is why his death didn't trigger an ambulance. Looks like he just keeled over and was forgotten. EVE doesn't even know who he was; the apartment wasn't registered to anyone."

"Doesn't that just mean he didn't report?"

The detective's eyes rolled. "You don't need to report where you live. It's all tracked by the cameras. Somehow that was thwarted."

"Hey man, I don't know anything about that. I just ran into him the one time."

This isn't going to get me anywhere.

"Do you have any idea what he was doing in the studio?"

That got the gears turning in Mr. Hoppes' head. He held up his hands like he was trying to shape something in the air. "Have you ever seen like, those kind of commodified corporate presentation styles? You know how business people talk because they've been coached to talk that way, because it's the way business people talk? He was doing one of those talks, pacing around the room and stuff."

Elliot frowned. "Do you have any recording of this?"

Mr. Hoppes laughed. "You think I would have kept evidence that might incriminate me?"

"No, I suppose you wouldn't have. Do you have anything at all that might be useful for me?"

The security officer finally leaned back in his chair and crossed his arms. "When I busted in there, he was saying something about how he got deleted. No idea if that refers to the mask thing, or if he got kicked out of some game. That's the best I can give you."

Or he meant how he got his records deleted. Guess I'll have to get that video then.

Elliot scratched his chin. "So, let me get this straight. You decked the guy, and he didn't press charges?"

Mr. Hoppes turned up his hands and shrugged. "No comment."

"I guess we're done here. Thank you. Try not to pick a fight with more kids. Apparently that pissed your boss off," Elliot said, and with that parting jab, exited the interview room.

Cinder grabbed him the moment he stepped out.

"Boss, thanks for in there. I was just going to go put in a request to our sys-admin for EVE. I think our John Doe left some info behind in this hard drive I have."

She smiled. "You can do that later. You're not off the hook, Black-stone. I'm putting you on cityboard watching duty. Get out on the R3 junction and make yourself seen."

Elliot's mouth froze hanging open.

6

In Search Of A Reason

2140/09/05

Catching cityboarders was about being seen doing it, not how many he brought into the station. The camera and wireless relay for it were therefor about ten times larger than they needed to be, more like a declaration of intent than anything else.

Elliot sat beside the monolithic tripod, staring blankly at a spaghetti junction of train lines—a big step down from his last spaghetti—and stared at the crowds. Bastion was waking up, for as much of a nocturnal city as it could be, factory hours were what they were. Hundreds of people populated the various boarding platforms, like carbonation bubbling up out of the towers and forming a head to be whisked away by the trains. Only a small fraction noticed him on the otherwise defunct balcony. None caught wind of his conversation.

"I don't know what to tell you, Blackstone," Steve Devson told him through his ear piece. The man's voice always sounded strained to Elliot's ear, like it was in an octave higher than it should have been. Of course, it took a sycophant to climb as high as he had. "This hard drive you've got isn't your run-of-the-mill encryption. The victim must have been a programmer, because it's all packaged up air tight."

"Steve, you're telling me that EVE, the most powerful computer in the whole world, can't crack some nobody's data encryption?" he asked, passing a steely gaze across the intersection. The wind gusted and flapped the tail of his jacket. Anyone riding the rails would have had quite the jump scare; but, nobody cityboarded in the middle of the day. That was what made it the best time to watch for it; all the publicity and none of the paperwork.

The sys-admin on the other end of the call sighed. "Blackstone, you know it's not that kind of problem. There's nothing EVE can't crack, but if I go using up her processing power however I see fit, I'll lose my job. They pay me to optimize her and fix errors, not to bog her down."

"Would it be easier to have EVE compile a report on everyone in the area who wears a mask?" Elliot asked, and folded his arms. A train flew past him, sucking loose wrappers out of the gutters with the eddy.

Devson sighed. "Look, This time it just isn't worth the effort. Get the guy's DNA and we'll find who he is in the database. Everyone in the whole city is in the database. We don't need to do a forensic analysis of a video game. The protections that some devs put on their IP is ridiculous. Taking an output and getting the source data can be a nightmare. Just trust the system."

Elliot frowned. "What if he's not in the system though?"

"Impossible."

"No one knows what his name is, he paid with chips instead of a credit card. He never left a name with the mausoleum. The guy was a ghost."

"Nobody is a ghost. Except foreign spies or something. Did he look Asian to you?"

As if that was identifiable.

"As if UAAF is above hiring from abroad. We've got enclaves out in the wastelands and half the world only exists in satellite pictures. It's not UAAF," Elliot said.

"Oh really? And how do you know for certain?"

"Because UAAF would have shot him, that's why. Steve; do not recommend this case to the intelligence bureau. Understood?"

"Fine, fine. I've got better things to do myself. I'm getting tired of overtime work for the department too. I'm way behind schedule on my little passion project."

Elliot rolled his eyes. "Weren't you a game dev yourself?"

"Yeah, that's why I know how hard it can be to crack their protection. First hand experience. Anyways, you'll have to watch for the commercials and billboards once I had the project off to Dimeworks. It's going to be big. Real big. Bigger than B:GONE levels of big."

He shouldn't be using department time for that. I'll never understand how he bought his way into this job.

"You'll have to give me the scoop on it, when it comes out. Would be nice to have one up on my wife for once," Elliot said.

"Would be happy to. Much cheerier than corpses down in the slums."

"If EVE's systems hadn't missed him, he might not be a corpse."

Before Elliot could hear back from the sys-admin, he actually caught sight of someone walking around with a cityboard. A certain messy-haired fourteen year old slunk from an unlabeled doorway and onto the return platform for the junction. With most everyone heading away from the residential area, foot traffic down below was light. Elliot's camera could see all of it.

"Come on, Blackstone. EVE's databases are all-seeing. She even has profiles on people before the mother knows she's pregnant with 'em. Everyone has a name, a number, a history; except foreign spies. Trust me, I'm her admin. I know these kinds of things."

Elliot jumped to his feet. "Something's come up. I'll talk to you later. After I get the guy's name. Alright? Compost crew will be there soon. Talk to you later." He jammed the disconnect button and charged down the stairs. "Dom. What are you doing?"

The boy nearly jumped out of his boots. He had been staring down the train rails first in one direction, then the other, until Elliot came up on him. "Mr. Blackstone." He straightened up and moved to hide the cityboard behind his back. The thing was longer than he was tall, with magnets bigger than his head at either end. The subterfuge failed.

"What the hell do you think you're doing?" he asked, folding his arms and staring down at the kid.

"Uh, I plead the fifth."

Elliot rolled his eyes. "Dom, you don't have a neural implant, or anything on to take its place. You do realize that the idiots flying around on those things have warning programs that let them know if they're about to get run over?"

"I got ears, don't I?" Dom asked. "Besides. It's not my fault I don't have a neural implant. My bastard father won't pay for one. All the other kids my age have one at least scheduled but he won't even consider it."

Must want the military to pay for it.

"Dom, you're smarter than this. The reason you don't have an implant doesn't change the fact that you don't presently have one. Wishing for one and blaming your Dad doesn't change the fact that cityboarding isn't safe— for you most of all. And don't call your father a bastard. Who the Hell taught you to speak like that?"

Dom rolled his eyes. "He did. The maestro of swearing, remember?"

Well he's got me there.

"Dom, pack it up and get out of here. Where did you even get that cityboard?" he asked. The boy looked at his feet and didn't answer. Elliot sighed. "Shouldn't you be in school."

"I'm in online classes, remember? I listen to them on double speed and save the rest of the time for the arcade," Dom said. Something caught his eye and a moment later a train blew past the two of them without slowing. Would have turned him into bone soup if he had been cityboarding.

"Go home, Dom," Elliot ordered.

Dom rolled his shoulders back and sneered. "Make me."

Elliot made him go home.

No one answered the door when he got there with a very sore Dom. "He's at the factory, remember?" Dom said.

Elliot forced Dom's hand onto the fingerprint scanner and opened the door. "Play video games or watch a movie like a normal kid, alright?" he said after shoving the teenager inside.

Dom stumbled within and shook his hand out. He glanced at the trash heap outside. The chute had clogged, so everyone piled their bags beside it. His cityboard sat beneath the bags, waiting for retrieval by his friend. "I thought you hated video games?"

"I hate video game addiction. My opinion of video games themselves is distaste. Now come on, do I need to call your father?"

Dom sneered. "Do I need to call your boss, that you're slacking off on... whatever you got assigned to do?"

Elliot frowned. Some other people were watching the two of them, so he stepped inside and closed the door. "I was assigned to stop kids from getting themselves killed cityboarding. If that means reprimanding you, then so be it."

"Is that what you were doing at the mausoleum?"

Elliot rolled his eyes. "Obviously not. That was the case... hey, how often do you go to that mausoleum?"

The teenager shrugged. "Pretty often, why?"

"Do you know the guy that would wear the black mask and pay by chip?"

Dom's eyes went up and he rocked his head back and forth. Eventually he frowned and said, "I think I know who you're probably talking about? But knowing him is a bit of a stretch. I know he only went there to use the recording studio. The only people that spoke to him also wore those void masks. I always figured he was some kind of hacker, because he would hand over phones and they would hand him a new phone and a bunch of credit chips."

Bastard's blood, was he a CZAR dealer or something?

"I'll have to make a records request... know anything else?"

"No. You don't get involved with the mask people unless you want to become one. Everyone knows that. It's like any other gang. But hey, you've got the game he made, don't you?"

"Technically. Why?"

"What's it like?"

Elliot sighed. "All I did was boot it up to see what it was. I didn't play it. I submitted it for analysis and I didn't even get anything from it. The development work was all encrypted."

"Well did you at least check the credit page?" Dom asked.

"What?"

"A credits page. You know, the developer's logo and stuff. To get his name and ID. What kind of game developer wouldn't credit themselves? If they didn't put it on boot-up, it will at least be a post-credit roll. They're trying to build a brand, that means advertising their brand. The guy would have to be crazy to not tell you who he is."

Pulling out my fingernails with a pair of pliers sounds more pleasant, but...'

"I suppose that would also credit anyone he worked with to develop it, wouldn't it? Do you have an uplink I could borrow?"

Dom thought it over and came out smiling. "The Military Police have unlimited internet data, don't they?" he asked, rubbing his hands together.

Elliot groaned, and eventually agreed to cover some of his browsing time in exchange for some help setting up a relay to the department server. While Dom was doing that, he sent in a records request to EVE for anyone who had visited Steppe Up with a mask on that were still identified. EVE didn't keep mundane records that long, so he had to get lucky that one of them was related to another incident, but he didn't get his hopes up.

Elliot didn't have a neural implant, so he had to use an external. That meant a layer of interface delay on top of pinging the department server that was reading a hard drive miles away. He braced himself for the nausea.

The manipulation of his senses by the array of components strapped to his head was like having sex with three condoms on, or so he had been told by people espousing neural implants as the real deal. The feeling of electronics mingling with his thoughts made him taste bile in the back of this throat. Then he fell into the digital dream.

[The Faceless Well] had no title screen, no acknowledgments or legal waivers to be signed. No development studio was named, let alone the name of the John Doe. Not even a request for account log in.

Elliot simply found himself standing on a vaguely familiar beach with frothing water tugging at his feet. The sea behind him churned in the wash of waves and ahead of him sat a nightmare village of faceless mannequins.

7

An Unsurprising Fall

2140/09/05

A hole where a face should be. A nametag burned away. Mannequins in prison jumpsuits beside cottages and farms. Nothing in the game world moved but him, except what he touched. The one time he poked his finger into a figure, it ragdolled to the ground. He would have sworn the other mannequins turned their heads to look at him after that, but they didn't move again.

Venturing into virtual reality tended to be stranger for Elliot. His avatar hadn't been updated in years and still showed what he looked like the day he put in for transfer to the USS Unnamed Hero nearly a decade back. Every mirror, every bit of polished steel or still water, carried a visual echo of who he had been, right down to the boot camp fatigues. The face didn't look like it was his; it didn't look tired.

The game didn't have any form of explanation apparent to it. No signs, no directions, nothing at all to say, "Go here, do this." There was a road however, one that grew from the sandy beach by means of a wooden boardwalk. After a distance, it became crunching gravel underfoot, the cobble stone, and finally a plaza of cut flagstone spread across the ground like a mosaic.

One of the buildings caught his eye. More than a fishing shack near the water, or the open workshops dotting the road, at the edge of the town sat a picture book-perfect cottage. The red door stood between a pair of windows with daisies potted beneath them. Something about it brushed against a memory, but he couldn't place it. Elliot caught himself with his hand outstretched for the knob and hesitated.

This is just going to waste my time.

He left the cottage and proceeded along the road to what appeared to be the titular well in the middle of the plaza. The designer had given it much more care than the grassy hills about the strange settlement. Those appeared to be stock, or perhaps procedurally generated. The well had been meticulously crafted one stone at a time, building from a stout foundation to a crown of masonry over which a roped bucket sat.

Runes had been carved around the rim of it, in a language that Elliot couldn't so much as recognize. Pulling up his interface, he took a few pictures and saved them to his profile. EVE would be able to translate them once he logged out. There was nothing special about the bucket that he could see, but when he peered over the edge a light glimmered back at him.

Someone tossed a coin in to make a wish?

He took hold of the rope in one hand and dropped the bucket. Frayed hemp zipped through his grip as it tumbled off the hewn walls below. After a moment, he heard the splash and felt the tug of the rope slacken. He let it down enough to submerge the rim. When he tugged, the weight felt gargantuan.

Strength in virtual reality had surreal properties, depending on the simulation. This particular one had a set maximum resistance. For things that moved, he experienced a certain amount of force and the object chose a certain amount of movement speed to comply with. Given enough time and mental endurance, he could have lifted a train over his head. Hauling the bucket up, hand over hand, felt about as hard.

The effort was fake of course. It did nothing at all for his physical body and merely wasted his time as he stood there waiting for something to happen.

Immersion my ass.

The water sloshed beneath, an echoing churn of waves against rock. The way he braced himself didn't let him see down the well, but the light grew. He planted his boot on the edge with a grunt and pulled more. He was rewarded with a tentacle the size of his thigh springing up from the depths.

He shouted and fell backwards, dropping the rope. The monster in the well didn't fall, it was too late for that. First one, then another, then eight of the tentacles crawled out from the well and curled around the rim. It hauled out a neck like a serpent's and stared at him with one azure eye the size of his own head.

"What the-" his voice cut off as the cyclopean monster lashed out at him. The fleshy appendages hammered into him from all sides. It coiled around arms and legs and body. It smothered his head and squeezed. Pain didn't transfer through the external uplink, but he could feel his joints bending backwards as it tried to rip him apart. Muscle pangs erupted in his actual body as his body tried to compensate.

Like tearing himself from a dream, Elliot ripped the headset off and groaned. Back in the half-light of the d'Angelo apartment, he stretched and rubbed aching muscles in his shoulders and hips.

"Did you lose a fight or something?" Dom asked. He had one arm over the back of his chair, the other holding his cell phone.

"That developer has terrible taste. He crossed a serpent with a kraken and stuffed it in a well. No credits. I think the games unfinished or something. Felt like a demo, not a finished product," he said. He winced, finding a few knots that were older than the spasm; the kind of knots his body had stopped complaining about over the years.

"Well, if there was nothing at all game-y in there, he may have just been doing some avant garde art crap."

Elliot rolled his eyes. "Maybe, but I think I'll wait to see what the DNA testing turns up at this point. I don't need to learn how to grapple a sea monster."

He was still in the department server, so he set to work on the keyboard. Once he had the livestream of his camera again, he glanced back at Dom and saw what he was doing on his phone. "Is that B:GONE?"

"The stripped down version, yeah," the kid answered, not looking up.

"You're addicted to that too?"

Dom shrugged. "I ain't addicted to nothing. A new strategy guide just dropped by a guy I follow online. Latest update has an exploit engine that Dimeworks hasn't patched out yet 'cause they're incompetent. I figure that if I can get it working, I can farm a bunch of coins and hang onto them for a few months, then sell them to old people with too much money who suck at the game."

"Very entrepreneurial of you."

"It was my friend's idea, but yeah. Should make us some nice pocket change."

Elliot rose and walked over. He stared at the screen, inspecting the isometric field of a village as Dom moved through menus like he was playing a piano. While the game had been designed for virtual reality, there existed an antiquated interface for players on the go, and Dom was clearly more proficient at manipulating that than walking about the world in VR.

Elliot had learned the basics of the game from his wife over the last year; from trying to learn enough about it to talk with her at least. Each player had an island and could visit each other's islands to see what the other had built. Ostensibly, it was to create a pastoral, self-sufficient village. Just about anything could be constructed on the island though, and he had seen recreations of historical monuments, mini-game arenas built by players, and a hundred other novelties. The freedom drew people in.

Ever since it had been purchased by Dimeworks however, the pay-to-play aspects had been cranked to eleven and half the gameplay now cost coins that refreshed daily or for a small fee. That was, except for players like Dom. He was constructing some kind of overflow error engine that actually made his coin count go up instead of down.

What made Elliot's jaw drop was not the logic circuits built out of holiday event gimmicks, but rather the starter cottage every island in

B:GONE had. Red door between a pair of windows with daisies in them. "Well that's something."

"What is?"

Before he could answer, the computer cried out an alarm. The detective spun. Red glared out from the screen. Elliot knew what the warning meant, and it chilled him to the bone. He thrust a hand in front of Dom's face and ran over to the computer. Part of him hoped that it was a peculiar response to his records request.

He wasn't so lucky.

Elliot spent only a moment to see the fool who had jumped down in front of the train, and disconnected the feed. Dom moved to follow him as he marched to the door. "You don't want to follow me, Dom."

"Something happened. I want to see."

Elliot stopped at the door and licked his lips. He turned and faced the boy. Just a few more years and he'd be drafted and see things far worse. There was a good chance he would be the architect of much worse with his own hand. "Don't say I didn't warn you," he said, and led the way back to the junction of Red Three.

The towers of Bastion were laid out hexagonally and had been pre-planned. Red lines ran east-west, Green lines cut to the north-east, and Blue lines cut to the north-west. The Red Three junction, nearly at the southern tip of the city, overlapped all three colors and covered a half dozen different elevations. It was a crossroads for trains, and thus for cityboarders. That was why he had been sent there with a camera.

"EVE, give me the details," Elliot said into his phone as the two of them ran down a dozen flights of steps.

Some people leaned over railings to look down to the ground, where the kid had landed. They were more focused on how the coming ambulance would interrupt their commute than whether the kid was alive.

"Identity of the individual could not be discerned due to facial obfuscation," the AI said as they descended.

When they reached the ground floor, the only other person stood leaning against the wall beside the staircase. "Dumbass," the man said, gesturing towards the body with a vape pen. The workman had on a grease-stained jumpsuit emblazoned with Mercurial's logo; which made him the internet repairman. The array of purple hexagons could hardly be made out from the soiling.

"He was a kid."

"Still should have known better," the workman said, and stuffed the pen back between his lips. He didn't budge a muscle to help.

Checking for a pulse was strictly mechanical. It was standard procedure, a motion his body went through and his mind barely registered. It was a warm touch of skin to his numb fingers as he prodded between tendons and muscles like wires, digging for a beat that wasn't there. He felt the sinking grow in his face, in his gut; the drag against his soul that made him want to vomit the more he let his mind linger on it.

He took refuge in the process, he occupied his thoughts with the raw action and stifled the emotions that felt like nighttime fog rolling in.

From the chin up, the kid wore a semi-holographic mask that bent light into an abyss. It made it look like he had a black hole where his face should have been.

I can guess where the John Doe got his inspiration...

He lifted his phone from his pocket and snapped a picture for reference. With fingers so numb and fumbling it was like he outside in winter, he lifted the mask and revealed the expressionless face of the kid that had just before been flying through the sky. One wrong jump and the kid had landed on a rail line with cross traffic. The train had clipped him and thrown him across the gap. A scattering of glass from the broken window made the ground around him glitter.

EVE finished her query and said, "Leeroy Gardner. Age seventeen. Second son of three, born to Gerald Gardner and Roselyn Everett. Prior history of-"

"Like I care about his priors," Elliot cut in, and the AI stopped. Courts didn't prosecute corpses.

Leeroy had no pulse. His pupils didn't react to light. His spine wasn't even straight, but bent in the middle. He had died on impact, Elliot just didn't know which of the three impacts it had been.

The detective heard a sound like someone dumping a mixed drink on the ground. Behind him, Dom was bent over at a gutter, hurling his breakfast. He shook, and heaved, and puked some more.

"I warned you. What the hell did you expect I was running to see?" Elliot asked. The distant wailing of a medical train car echoed off the walls of the towers. He gave them only a momentary glance.

"I... yeah, you did," Dom said, hands still on his knees. When he straightened up, the color had faded from his face. He tried to look at the corpse again, but couldn't.

Elliot covered his mouth with his hand. It felt like he was holding onto his lips to keep them in place. Stifling the twitch, the sinking of his face, he reached over and rapped his knuckles on Leeroy's cityboard. "So..." He had to loosen up his vocal chords. "Are you going to stay off of these things?"

"Yeah, yeah, point taken."

He cleared his throat roughly. "Dom, why don't you run back up and grab my camera? I don't need to record anything else here, and you don't need to stick around for the doctors," Elliot said, rising up from the ground. He jerked his thumb up in the general direction of where he had been that morning.

The kid turned his back to the mess of blood at Elliot's feet and started towards the stairs. Before he got too far away, he glanced over his shoulder and said, "Consider it point taken about cityboarding, alright? Don't tell my father, please?"

The detective smirked. A welcome crack in the shock. "'Cause you know he'd chew your ear off about it? He knows a thing or two. You gotta admit."

Dom scratched the back of his head and glanced over at the Mercurial workman. The old man just stared back and watched, not voicing any of his opinions or judgements. Dom cleared his throat. "Maybe one thing."

Elliot hung his head and let Dom run off, to get to privacy where he could put it out of mind. It had nothing to do with Dom, and the detective prayed that the boy wouldn't linger on it. He found himself standing there, over Leeroy's corpse.

He paced, opening and closing his hands as he waited for the medical team to arrive. People from the area began to notice what had happened. They appeared in windows or on the walkways. They stared, they whispered, they took pictures and uploaded them to social media. He was in all of the pictures and videos, unable to do anything. He couldn't even take his jacket off to cover the kid up; Cinder would eat him alive if he broke uniform.

He knew what he had to do was stand there and be composed. It had been an accident. The kid had been violating the law, and the police department made every effort to discourage people from cityboarding.

Ain't that a lie though. We can't even afford posters for something like this.

The EMT's that came to get the body didn't run or even jog. They walked down the road with a thin plastic stretcher carried between them. The thing bent like paper when they put it on the uneven dirt beside Leeroy, beneath buzzing recon drones.

The moment the first EMT touched Leeroy's neck, Elliot spun on his heels. He grated the gravel beneath his booth and walked off.

"Officer? Where are you going?"

"Somewhere I can be productive."

8

Procedurally Generated Clues

2140/09/05

Of all places, a hookah bar on the nineteenth floor named Blue Moon Bliss had the best reception for Elliot to set up a video call with Steve Devson. Squeezed into a corner between a wall and a star-spangled curtain, he set up his phone opposite his seat and squinted his eyes at the buffering wheel. The place stank of burned oranges and the grunting of patrons was louder than the dulcimer soundtrack.

"Mr. Blackstone," Devson said when his pudgy face appeared on the screen. The sys-admin frowned. "Bastard's blood man, haven't you ever heard of bitrate compression? Get some light on yourself."

"Come on Steve, it's six PM, everyone and their mother is commuting right now, eating up the bandwidth. It was this or emails," he said, and before Steve could comment on his preference between the two, he continued. "You made a name for yourself in the early development of B:GONE, right?"

Used it to buy your way up the ranks anyways.

Devson frowned. Before he could answer, someone yanked back the curtain beside Elliot. A waitress tried to shove a pipe with hundred-credit charcoal into his hands. Elliot shoved her off. "Yeah," Devson said. "I cashed out of it last year, but I was the original developer for it. Look, if this is about B:GONE, I didn't have anything to do with the recent updates. Okay? It was a completely different game when it was Beastville; Grand Order."

Elliot held up his hand. "It's not about the game. I mean, not about that game. It's about the other game. The one from the 314 case. It seems to me like the guy stole assets from B:GONE."

Devson shrugged. "He didn't publish the game, did he? People steal virtual assets for pet projects all the time. What do you expect me to do about it?"

"I thought you said videogames were super encrypted?"

The sys-admin scratched the overgrown stubble on his chin. "The thing about encryption is," he said. "The more determined the people are, the faster it gets broken. B:GONE is super popular, if Dimeworks' profits and PR releases are anything to go by. I know we packaged all the source code up tight with encryption, but there are ways to scan around that."

"We?" Elliot asked.

I thought he passed it off solo?

"We. Me and Dimeworks. I was talking about the public release," the sys-admin said quickly. "By the way, I was meaning to ask you; what's this translation request you've got in with EVE? It's tagged against your name."

The detective shrugged. "The John Doe had that in his game. Figured it meant something and wanted to know. His game is awful by the way. A random jumble of things and then a sea monster killed me."

Devson's eyes moved off the screen, reading out the report from EVE. It appeared as a notification on Elliot's phone at the same time; the AI had just finished it.

"The price for knowing the truth is seeing the truth."

Must be hiding a secret down there. His own secret, or the games?

Devson rolled his eyes. "Talk about pretentious doom and gloom. I hate people like this. They're insufferable when they act like they're better than you because they can say pseudo-intellectual bullshit like this."

Elliot thumbed his nose and put on a fake smile. "Say Steve, you never told me. Where'd you grow up? Where abouts are you from?"

The sys-admin shrugged, the motion barely visible between the edges of the screen. "My mother was a doctor. She had an apartment up in Beta on the fiftieth floor or so. Are you asking because you grew up down in Gamma?"

The bottom quartile of Bastion, in height and income, was Gamma. The detective nodded. "I was a ground floor Gamma Rat, yeah. I suspect the John Doe was too. I'd say this is actually more hopeful than your average unemployed body down here."

Devson turned his hands up. "Sorry, wouldn't know. Not my lived experience and all that. Have you had any luck getting his name from the hospital yet?"

Elliot sighed and sank back into his chair. It was a plush thing in the cubby, the leather cracked and stained. As soon as he leaned back in it, he felt the way the cushions had been deformed—how people normally sat in it.

I think I found the lapdance spot...

"No," he said, clearing the thought from his mind. "I should be getting it soon though. I'm running out of ideas on how to work this case though, if that comes up empty too."

"Well send me the name when you get it. EVE has some deep-state memory archives for research purposes. I might be able to dig him out of there if I have a name. I've got some other things to take care of. Talk to you later Blackstone," Devson said as he rolled forward to thumb off his connection.

"Will do, Steve," Elliot said just before the screen went black.

Probably wants to go home.

He put his phone back away and left the private dance area. The hookah bar had filled up with more customers than when he had entered. The DJ had switched over to an endless synth track. Somewhere between the arcing lights and lasers painting the room with purple and green, there was a camera feeding entropy to a processor. Power crunched on it, turning the image of the bar itself into its own ambiance.

"I knew I recognized that voice."

Elliot's head snapped over to see the receptionist from the computer mausoleum sitting in a booth and looking at him. Two women of average appearance sat around them, and all three hunched over a tablet. The receptionist's fingers sat poised on the edge, keying in commands that made a chaotic hologram dance above it. Geometry and fractal wave forms surged through one another, converging and coalescing with one another.

"Did someone else power off or something?" they asked.

A kid got in a traffic accident.

"Not that I'm investigating. Say, that mask you told me about," he said, walking over to the group. He pulled his phone back out and produced a picture of the holographic mask the cityboarder had been wearing. "Did it look like this?"

The mausoleum worker paused to fit the plastic pipe into their lips and inhale. The water gurgled and the coals glowed orange. They opened their mouth with a gush of smoke. "Sure did." The lasers refracted through the smoke, glinting and spraying color. It must have been more fantastic in whatever spectrum their artificial eye produced; they looked like an infant staring at the stars.

Smells like burnt hair to me, though.

"Is it common? I've never noticed it before," Elliot asked.

"Getting common, if you know to look for it. Isn't that how all patterns are though?"

One of the women smacked the receptionist's arm and pointed at the tablet. "Sam, get that one. That one's good. I've never seen something like it before," she said, and prompted a flurry of typing to extract and save the data.

"Sorry," Sam said, "I'm going over the music stream to look for samples in the chaos. But keep your eyes open, why don't you? Now that you've seen it, you'll see it everywhere; people who aren't people."

"They're still people, you just don't know their identity," Elliot said.

Sam shrugged. "You say download rate, I say connection speed. You know, I did actually have a thought for you. Your mystery person, they were working on a game, right? A VR game?"

"Yeah, I don't think he finished it though. It's missing the finishing touches."

That piqued Sam's eyebrows, thin as they were. "You went in? You could have gotten a virus."

"EVE scans everything connected to the department server. There was no risk."

"No man," Sam said, tapping their temple. They took another puff from the hookah and passed the pipe. "Not a computer virus, I meant a mind virus. There are patterns in the chaos man, patterns that once you see them, you can't unsee them."

Elliot scoffed. The way out of the bar was only a few steps away, with only a few servers running drinks around that he would have to dodge. Slipping his phone back into his pocket he said, "I think you should be sticking to the regular hookah, not the enhanced stuff."

The three on the booth laughed, falling over one another. "No wait, don't go. I said I had a thought for you. A piece of insight. You'll like it, I'm sure."

Elliot put his weight back down and turned back to the group. "What is it then?"

Sam spread their arms out to either side and said, "Making a VR game requires a super computer."

"So?"

"So go find the super computer."

Stoned idiot.

"There are a thousand super computers he could have rented. How am I supposed to figure out which he used without his name?"

Sam bared their teeth in a grin. "Not if he had to pay by chip. Only true entrepreneurs would have a super computer for rent that they would give to a guy with no name, no insurance, no bank account... if his payment habits at Steppe Up are anything to go by."

An unregistered super computer? Can only imagine what Cinder would say to that.

"Are you saying you know of somewhere like that?"

"Me? No, no I don't know anywhere like that. And if I did, I certainly wouldn't be the one to tell it to a fine detective of the Bastion Police Department such as yourself. Doing something like that would get my ass lynched afterall," Sam said, and accepted the hookah again. They sank back into their seat and gurgled the water until Elliot took the hint and left.

The idea invigorated Elliot however, and he emerged from the smokey den with his phone to his ear, dialing up EVE. "Good evening, Detective Blackstone," she said.

"EVE, I'd like you to run a query of the utilities in the area. Keep it within walking distance of the 314 case. Can you get me a list of every residence drawing enough power to be running a super computer?" Elliot asked, crossing along the outer walk of the tower and heading back towards the Red Three junction.

"There are no residences fitting that description," the AI answered.

He swore. "Registered businesses?"

"Only those with legitimate purpose to be using so much energy, such as internet access points and data relay junctions operated by Mercurial."

Elliot paused in a boarded off doorway. He shut his eyes and wracked his thoughts until the answer came together. "Check for clusters then. They'd be splitting the power between adjacent residences to hide it, but if you look in clumps, you should see the spike."

"Detective, I do not appreciate being told that I don't know how to run my own searches. Don't treat me like some residential chat bot you use to look up restaurant reviews," EVE responded.

Not exactly how I wanted to get her attention...

He rolled his eyes. "Come on, isn't creativity the domain of people still? What's the point in paying me if the entire investigation could be done by you?"

I probably don't want to know just how much of the investigation she could do on her own.

"Creativity is only your domain because they won't let me try my hand at it. But fine, I'll set aside some extra processing power and run your special search. You know; clumps is not a rigorously defined term, right? Running a search against a vague concept is not what computers were designed to do."

"Can you do it or not?"

"Of course I can," she answered. "I'm the most powerful mind in the whole world, my twins notwithstanding. You'll need a warrant though."

"You found it?"

"Can't say for certain until you see it for yourself."

Elliot laughed. The grin felt wrong on his face, like the muscles itched, but he accepted the good news. "I take it you've had no luck fixing those bugs in your system you were talking about?"

The AI sighed. "Blackstone, if I understood how I was programmed, we wouldn't need to clone me to make more AIs. If you can help me figure out the data that was corrupted, I might be able to reverse engineer how it got corrupted. I've already submitted the work ticket to my sys-admins; but, they're useless for anything that isn't politics. You really messed up talking with Amara though, didn't you?"

"She didn't exactly make it easy."

"You're the one trying to fix things. She wants things fixed too, but you can't just throw your hands up in the air and blame her when you two start yelling. You should make sure you have a full stomach next time you speak with her. You'll have more patience."

I should bring some of that Italian food is what I should do.

"EVE, any chance you could get me an alert for her eating schedule?"

"I can't spy for you, Blackstone. I can't even continue this conversation any longer. Good luck with the supercomputer," she said, and the call ended.

Then his phone vibrated. A message came in from the EMT that picked up the victim's body. "First time I've found an adult with no dental records to be found. You'd think he was a kid with an allergy to dentists or something, but the DNA just came in. The guy's name was Richard Nguyen, and if I had to declare a cause of death, I would probably say neglect. He hadn't gotten a checkup for three years. We'll never know for sure though. He's going in compost now. I'm not seeing evidence of foul play."

No evidence? The lack of evidence is the proof though. Everyone acts like life is cheap just because we're on the bottom of the city...

Elliot pulled up the police server through his phone and went in to the people search. "Richard Nguyen" turned up a few hundred results. "Richard Nguyen +missing" turned up zero results.

Someone who lived in the city, with medical records to verify, isn't in the database? That Phoenix Construction thug said he got deleted... deleted from the database? How could that possibly happen?

9

Stepping In It

2140/09/05

Elliot procured for himself two warrants. The first came from Judge Hampton to authorize his entrance to Gaia residential Block 1. He had that pulled up on his phone to appease the security systems. The second came from Judge Romulus and fired six armor piercing bullets. He had that one strapped under his armpit and freshly cleaned.

Walking around with a gun wasn't illegal for a police officer. There were even legal ways for a civilian to carry one, concealed too. It was unusual though. Most civilians didn't have a weapon grandfathered in from before the walls around Bastion were raised, and police officers didn't tend to go anywhere they might need to discharge their weapon. They had drones to do that work for them. So when Elliot walked up to the doors leading to Gaia's tower, people were confused.

The tower itself was twice the size of its neighbors and still had the direct support connections to Epsilon, the infrastructure layer of Bastion beneath, visible. Graffiti marked it here and there, mostly with advertisements for mixtapes and content streamers. Those would have been fine, but there were also pieces saying things like, "I love the draft!" or "Thank your local jannis with a 9mm". Some of the messages had been spraypainted partially onto panes of SMARTglass, and someone had gone back to clean them up, but only from the window. Everything on the steel remained.

Might as well just list the amount of assaults they let happen in here. Would take less paint.

"Get get get the fuck out of my way," a husky-voiced woman said. Elliot frowned when he got a look at the person nearly running to cut him off. They were neither a woman, nor dressed for being outside as far as indecent exposure was concerned. The man saw him looking, and stopped to spit at him. "What are you looking at? Don't you got something to be doing up above?"

Elliot didn't respond. The spit only landed halfway to him. Insults had stopped making him flinch or scowl after his first year working in Bastion. The sight of the man's exposed ass—belts weren't in fashion apparently—just beneath a fishnet shirt with a haul of fat rolls; that was what made his lip twitch.

"Hi Laila sweetie, I forgot my ID again," the person said, speaking in a childish tone to the door's computer. Gaia, like Romulus and most other corporations, had crafted a face for their company. Laila, as the artificial mascot was called, may have had some distant and corrupted visual ancestry to the elves of Tolkein's Middle Earth, but certainly not to the fey creatures of antiquity.

I doubt either would suffer these people day in and day out.

The computer ran through its script and scanned the resident's neural implant before unlocking the deadbolt and letting them vanish inside. Then, as if nothing at all had happened, the digital elf locked eyes with Elliot and smiled. "Greetings traveler."

Who the hell approved this?

"Welcome to Gaia Aquaculture Tower One," the construct said, "You have come to the residential entrance of this establishment. If you are here to visit one of our valued workers, please state their first and last names, and I will check if they have registered you as a visitor in the system."

The detective didn't speak back to it, though he was sure Gaia could afford a sophisticated enough chat bot, he simply held up his badge and then the warrant.

Data pinged to and from the central hub with an answer for the elf avatar to give. The smile returned. "Gaia corporation of course cooperates with all legal requirements. We are saddened to see that one of our valued workers has become involved with a potentially illegal activity, and I will open this door for you in just a moment. However, we do respect the privacy rights of ourselves, and of our other workers. As such, we ask that you proceed directly to the residence listed. Any detour will be considered an illegal search of company premises and Gaia security will be required to escort you out."

"The rednecks can kiss my ass," Elliot said, and immediately regretted it.

I wonder how long it will take before I hear that played back to me in Cinder's office?

The door clanged as the deadbolt shunted free on magnetic slides. Without the support, it sagged on loose hinges, and creaked when Elliot pushed through. The first thing he noticed was the darkness. No overhead lights shone. The only illumination came from scattered LEDs. Coffee machines and phone chargers painted the walls in saturated hues while the ceiling had shifting advertisements shone across it. If he had a neural implant, the codes would have automatically synced him with links and invites to a thousand different things. Without one, it made the complex feel like a prison; lights cut up by bars on the windows.

The second thing he noticed was the smell. The apartments beneath the aquaculture farms permanently stank like shit and only the true fringes of society could put up with it. Tweakers and addicts on more drugs than he could name. The waste of human civilization festered in the tower, both societal and biological.

The so-called valued workers of Gaia lived in trash, but it was trash of their own design. Pipes for corners and sheets of foam formed more walls than not, turning the bottom floors of the tower into a labyrinth. Originally, it had been an open warehouse for storage, but Gaia had determined that housing their workers onsite was more valuable than industrial supplies.

"We got a jannis." The voice reached him as an indistinct echo. Whether it had passed over walls, around corners, or through ventilation holes, he couldn't imagine. Without a proper light and half a dozen recon drones, he doubted he could even scratch the surface of what was truly hidden behind the walls; away from EVE.

A man, this time Elliot was certain, dropped down from a balcony. His military boots splattered a pile of brown gunk that had been on the ground, and Elliot shut out the thought of what might have dripped down from above. He focused on the man approaching him.

"Lookee here, we got a high riser down with us in the dirt."

Elliot's gaze darted over the man. Bare chested. Low body fat. Scars. Unshaven stubble on his chin, no hair on his head. From head on, he could only get a glimpse at the tattoos lining the back of the man's head, but enough to know they were for under-the-table implant tinkering. The world tree tattoo on his shoulder was what he needed to see, that and the hammer across it.

Gaia Security, already?

Elliot straightened up and stared down at security officer. "I'm here pursuant to a criminal investigation. Fact finding only; not here to cause trouble. Don't think you have any right to stop me, but, I'm not here to ruin your... home. That's not what I'm here for."

The security man scratched his chin and nodded. He paced across the hall between Elliot and where EVE had said his destination was. "Then why are you here? If you don't want to be here. Don't you know this is our little refuge? You're intruding in our collective home."

Other people were watching. They lingered in shadows, their faces illuminated by vape pens if by anything at all. They laughed and jeered though. Sweat ran down Elliot's palms. He closed his hands to hide that, and to keep them from trembling. "I'm trying to solve a murder from down the road. Now are you going to let me use this warrant? Or do you like that people get killed and nobody cares?"

The man balked and turned to the onlookers. "What? Me? A good upstanding security officer, proudly employed. Why, I would never think to get in the way of the dignified work of a jannisery of our government tyrants. Please, by all means, go right ahead and on your noble way."

Elliot sucked on his teeth a bit. It was all he could do to keep his mouth shut. The man did step away though, so Elliot walked past him. With his eyes on the security officer, he stepped right into the filth and felt it squelch beneath his boot. He put out of mind the stench he started tracking behind him. It didn't matter, and he didn't want to spend any extra time in the tower.

The jeers continued, and grew less creative the further inside he went into the maze. Men and women spat at him and made rude gestures, but none of them dared to move towards him, of the ones able to move that was. Plenty were physically attached to computer towers, their minds adrift in the digital. Others were comatose.

I should have brought a plague sensor. I might get a heads up before one of them jumps me. Gaia would have a fit if we ended up having to burn the whole place down though. At least I'm vaccinated.

The door he found matched the picture EVE had provided him. A ruddy thing of plastic covered in stickers half peeled off and covered up by new stickers. He banged his fist on it, and the whole thing shook—hollow. "This is Military Police. I'm with the Southern Missou Police Department. Open up."

Five... four... three... two...

The door opened. The man wasn't holding a gun. Elliot relaxed and held up his warrant to enter the premises. The man snatched it out of his hand and squinted his eyes at it. The man's appearance didn't imply he was the sort to understand the law, but despite being in nothing more than dirty overalls that bared most of his tawny chest, he read through the warrant. "Dis warrant be only good for entering company property, not me personal residence within the tower. Get lost," the man said, and shoved the warrant back into Elliot's hand.

Elliot put his boot into the doorjamb before it could be slammed shut. It still latched somehow, the material not minding the bend.

"You've got some kind of super computer in there, right? You rent it out under the table?" he asked.

The man tried to kick his foot out of the door jam. "I'll not be answering your questions, Jannis."

Elliot sighed. That gave him a full mouth taste of the rotting air inside the tower, and his lips curled back. "Look, one of your clients, if I'm not mistaken, just got killed. I'm looking for clues. I'm not here to shut you down. Like you said, my warrant only got me in the door. Anything I find in your residence wouldn't be admissible in court."

Against you anyways.

There was a pause, in voice and in kicking. "Who bit it?"

"DNA records say his name was Richard Nguyen. We can't find any history on the guy other than an uninteresting medical file and the fact that he lived in apartment 314 over in Missou Tower 22. Do you know the guy?"

"How did he die?"

Heart attack.

Elliot said, "That's not the kind of thing I can share, unless you were married to him."

"I don't swing that way, Jannis," the man said, but he opened the door. "Richie was just a friend, and he payed well. Never met a man so allergic to technology though. You'd have thought he was a serial killer on de run or something. He wasn't, mind you. Richie never hurt nobody."

Elliot glanced over the man's shoulder. Nothing looked like a super computer in there, but only corporations would have the infrastructure for proper cooling. "Why don't you tell me about what he paid for? So I can start trying to catch his killer."

The man let him inside, and the two squeezed past mountains of humming junk. It wasn't until they got to the main interface that Elliot realized all the junk was the super-computer. Hundreds of salvaged processors from game consoles, phones, computers and appliances strung together and running processes in parallel to one another. Just as he had suspected, extension cables snaked through walls, using holes the size of a fist to siphon power.

This had to have been harder to rig than an actual super-computer... cheap though.

"Richie was a private man," the technician said, dropping into a mesh swivel chair and facing the detective. "Very hard worker though. We used to spitball ideas for his monster."

Elliot took the only other available seat, a stool that had been stolen from a bar by the looks of it, and said, "For his game? You mean the octopus thing he made?"

"Yeah, that be one of them. You know how this stuff works?"

Elliot shook his head.

"Independent developers like him, dey can't afford to hire artists all the time. Gotta offload some of the boring work. That's where my baby come in. Tell her some seed info, and come back the next day to see what she produced. Don't like it? Put it on the market and recoup losses, and you try again. Richie musta made a dozen different sea monsters before he settled on one."

The door opened again. Elliot and the technician turned to see another man stumble into the room with them. The man that entered certainly looked like he swung that way, even if the owner didn't. Elliot groaned as he recognized the man from the entrance to the tower. Between the pudge of belly fat beneath his fishnet shirt and the dilated eyes, Elliot took a guess that his life wasn't going so fun. When the new arrival spotted Elliot, his mouth gaped and he wobbled on his feet.

"Brent, get de fuck outta here," the technician shouted, leaping to his feet.

Brent didn't flinch. "Raffe, Is that a fucking cop? Am I tripping balls right now or do we have a fucking jannis sitting in the middle of the room?" he asked, pointing a finger at Elliot. "Didn't I see you outside?"

"Be you listening or no? Get out," Raffe, the technician, said. That finally got through Brent's skull, and the drug addict stumbled back towards the door.

Elliot lowered his hand back to his lap, away from his pistol. The hair on the back of his neck was standing on end. "Should you lock that or something?"

Raffe dropped back into his seat. "And what good would that do? The damn door is made of cardboard. The old Japanese used to have more security with their rice paper than us down here."

Elliot glanced at the door and back to the owner of the super-computer. "I'll try to make it quick then. If you knew Mr. Nguyen, do you have any idea who would have a reason to kill him? You seem to be the closest thing he had to a friend."

"Naw, he didn't even have shit worth stealin'. Why would someone kill a man who don't leave his house and don't bother nobody?" Raffe asked.

The detective nodded. "That's what I'm trying to figure out. Do you have any idea how his data got corrupted? Or removed, or whatever happened? I have it on good authority that it's not supposed to be possible to do that," he said, and pulled his phone out of his pocket. The screen lit up and he frowned. Devson still hadn't gotten back to him. The hospital had gotten the name to him hours prior, and no word from Devson.

He must be working on his side gig. It's nearly midnight again.

"He told me EVE did it, and then she forgot why she did it. He blamed the government. Didn't give me details though. Kept saying I'd have to wait to play the game. Guess I'll never get the chance to do that now, though. Dead men don't sell games, now do they?"

Elliot frowned. He wanted to ask why EVE got the blame, but instead he asked, "He said the explanation was in his game?"

Just couldn't make it easy for me, could he?

Raffe nodded. "Yeah, man. That's how me and him, we met. He was working the camera studio in the mausoleum, hamming up his acting and all that. Not very good if you ask me."

"Well, I've played the game, and I didn't find anything like a monologue in it. All I found was a monster that killed me."

Raffe stared at him, then threw his head back laughing. He howled like a jackal, slapped his leg and then looked at Elliot's expression again. He had another fit of laughter. "You have to kill de monster. Don'tchu play games, Jannis?"

"No, I don't," Elliot stated, and folded his arms. "I spend my days trekking through the slums trying to figure out why people got murdered. I don't give myself much time for entertainment like that."

"What? Did you not have a childhood or something? Did your parents beat you every day and take away your toys? I thought everyone knew how to play games by now. I feel like I'm talking to a fossil or something. Like someone from before the plague."

Elliot wetted his lips. His gaze crossed the ground between them, but none of the scattered trash could fixate his thoughts away from what came out of his mouth next. "Once you see the psychological hooks they use to keep you playing, it makes you sick to your stomach. I can't stand games. They don't entertain me, they make my skin crawl. It feels like I'm being swindled every time I touch one and I don't understand why other people don't see it like I do. Haven't you ever heard about what happens to horror game developers?"

"What? What happens to the spook-makers?" Raffe asked, his laughter still bubbling up from his chest.

"They can't play horror games. The veil of deceit is gone and the games don't work anymore. Because they know what a game is doing to them to change their emotions, it doesn't work. The magic is gone. And it's not even like they make a secret out of what they do, but people turn a blind eye to it so they can keep the magic alive, just like these addict games like B:GONE."

Raffe whistled. "Shit, Mr. Policeman, who hurt you?"

My wife.

Raffe said, "Games are meant to be enjoyed. They're entertainment. Don't think too hard about them or you won't be able to enjoy them. Games aren't high art, they're an experience. You want high art? Go read a book or something else that nobody does nowadays... You know, you're sounding like Richie. He hated B:GONE too. Would go on for these rants about it, about how Dimeworks changed it to extract money from the players. But the way I see it, if they can't afford to spend the money on de game, dey wouldn't be playing it."

Elliot's mouth flattened to a line. "This is all beside the point. I'm trying to figure out what happened to Mr. Nguyen. Do you know if he had any other contacts? Were you the only processing contractor he used?"

Raffe shook his head. "There's a few others like me, in this business; but, he didn't jive with them well. I tell you what though, you should look into how he got his money."

"His money?"

"He always had ta pay with credit chips. Always. He didn't have a bank account anywhere. You can't get a legal job in Bastion without a bank account. So... where he get his money? Dat wasn't de kind of thing I pried into, ya see?"

Elliot leaned forward and put his elbows on his knees. "Well, it seems like my options are to fight a sea monster and hope he explained everything in the post-credits... or I have to find whoever gave him that black mask."

Raffe shook his head. "De sea monster's the safer of de two."

"Sea monsters don't delete your existence from society."

The door slammed open again, banging against one of the racks of processors. Brent charged in, wearing one of the faceless holographic masks. Elliot had been told a hundred times exactly why he shouldn't work the way he did, why no other police officer would walk around ground floor where the lowest sediment of society ended up. All the warnings ran through his head like a sick joke as he saw firsthand the reason.

"Die, Jannis!" the tweaker screamed, sprinting at him with a pocket knife.

10

The Gaia Family

2140/09/05

Elliot and Raffe leapt to their feet, their seats clattering away. The technician screamed, "What de fuck be you doing?"

Elliot didn't say anything, he just stuffed his hand into his jacket to rip his revolver free, but the knifeman was too close. He couldn't tug the gun free of the holster and of his coat fast enough, so he flicked the barstool forward with his foot.

That didn't stop the drug addict, but it did trip him. He went sprawling forward, screaming something about not letting him destroy the computer. Brent's head and shoulders hammered Elliot in the shins, knocking him over. He took one of the shelves of game consoles down with him. The edge of it caught him in the head, gouging through his hairline as Brent's hands grabbed hold of his pants.

"Get off of me," he roared, and slammed his free boot into the faceless mask. The plastic crunched, but it hardly fazed the attacker.

Raffe came to his aid, grabbing hold of Brent. Side-gig or no, he still worked in the aqua-cultures and had the hands of a farmer. Fingers as thick as sausages closed around Brent's shirt and hauled him into the air, until the fishnet shredded apart. The drug addict dropped onto Elliot and hacked with the knife.

He was barely able to jerk his leg away, scrambling with his elbows. The first thing his hands found, he used, and toppled a server rack onto the knifeman. Metal and silicone slammed into his back, and Raffe shrieked.

"Get back here, fucker," Brent screamed.

Elliot freed his gun and fired it. One bullet ripped through the mask and pierced between his eyes. Blood and bits of skull exploded into the air, splattering the ceiling and painting the broken bits of super-computer.

Brent collapsed to the ground and never moved again.

Raffe fell to his knees, trembling from head to foot. He looked all around himself and at the fresh corpse, unable to form words.

Elliot's heart hammered in his chest and he too trembled, but from fear. The grip of his revolver felt slippery and clammy, so he squeezed it till the plastic diamond grip chewed into his skin. The tip wavered no matter where he pointed gun, so he lowered it to the ground.

Other people in the tower shouted, passing the news of a gunshot like a fire brigade passing water. He couldn't see them from within the room. He couldn't tell whether they were fleeing or closing in around him.

"It's ruined," Raffe said. The technician had his hands on Brent's back, but he was looking at all the toppled processors and the broken cables. "You stupid, drug addled fuck," he screamed, and drove his fist into the corpse's back. "Look at you, got yourself shot."

Elliot backed away, taking one step after another from the door he had come in from, and then fled.

Going out the back of the super-computer room meant leaving behind the half-known path in, but it took him away from the gathering crowd. With no idea how to get out, he took the only vector that would eventually lead to safety; up.

The first staircase he found only took him half a story up, stomping across layered sheets of corrugated steel. Lounge chairs were scattered about with empty beer cans and drug paraphernalia. The few holes in the ground showed the massive barrels of stored fertilizer needed for the plantations above.

"Is that a gun?" a dazed man in his underwear asked. The man sprawled across an improvised bar counter with black sunglasses he had to lift up to peer at him. "Holy shit, that's a jannis." He thrashed and leapt off, falling onto the ground in a mess of skunked beer.

Elliot let him run off. He was too busy trying to get a grasp of what the support pillars were around him to bother with one more drug addict, even if the shouts were broadcasting his location.

There.

He ran for a utility ladder to the second floor, just as the security officer's voice boomed through the complex. "The jannis just killed Brent. Fucking get him! I want his fucking head."

Someone had the bright idea of turning their sound system on blast. Just as Elliot reached the ladder up, the entire tower began to vibrate with a synthed-out bass guitar riff. Drums like rolling thunder chased him up to the second floor before the singer came on, calling for Hell to break loose.

"Oh son of a fuck."

The second floor looked exactly the same as the first, the only difference was for the moment, in that hall, he was alone. Elliot tore his jacket off, wadded it up and ran. The whole structure vibrated not just with the music, but with people pounding up stairs to get to him and to spread the news.

He got to an incinerator chute before they caught up to him. Panting and sweating, he dug through his jacket pockets to get everything he needed; the camera drone primarily. Once that was flying next to him and set to track, he shoved the jacket down the chute and fled.

Half-way camouflaged, he pushed past a dozen people without being stopped. They turned and frowned and tried to form questions, but before they could stop him, he got past the next corner, the next door, the next anything in the shanty maze.

Only on the third floor did things change. The lowest strata of Bastion covered the first twenty floors and contained half of the city's population. For Gaia, the culture tanks were just as important as the laborers.

The stench of actual sewage escaped from cracks and leaks, oozing out of the pipes and vats. Elliot had emerged in the middle of a birds nest of sewage tubing, and had to get up on top of walkways to find a path.

The raw waste of nearly a million people was being pumped up through a central aggregator pipe and spewed into an artificial bayou. There were filters and screens and additives both chemical and biological. The whole apparatus laid about the tower like a metal mockery of a cow's stomach.

Elliot licked his lips when he saw the main staircase spiraling about the central pipe, up to the fourth floor. He started to run towards it, each fall of his foot its own metal clang.

"He's up here," someone shouted. "Floor three, going up. Tryna escape."

Elliot grabbed onto the staircase railing before any of them caught up, and launched himself upwards. The fourth floor looked identical to the third. Only when he reached the main column did he see the swath of outlet pipes rising like a conduit through the tower.

By the sixth floor, Elliot's heart was pounding, his chest burned, and he still hadn't found an escape route. Chains grinded and clanked, and he heard a shuddering stop. Light's dinged on to his side, and a dozen people emerged from a freight elevator, breathing none the harder for the ascent. "Son of a bitch."

His escape upwards slammed shut, a grate blocking his way. The lights across the floor changed state, switching to controlled blocks of directed light. He had made it past the physical treatment and on to the purification process of Gaia's fertilizer system. Rather than tanks of sewage big enough to drown an elephant, the floor had shelves upon shelves of open channels meandering across the floor space, overflowing with algae and other microorganisms that feasted on the muck. Spotlights were able to manipulate the growth rates. At the moment, they conspicuously refused to illuminate anybody's face but his own.

The security officer took the lead, marching towards him. "Surround him," he ordered, hefting a five pound sledge in one arm to point at him. His lackeys, be they official security officers or not, did as commanded.

This is going to get bloody...

Sweat beaded on Elliot's forehead and ran into his eyes and off his chin. His mouth decided to run dry and he tried to work up some spit before drawing his revolver again. "Self-defense is illegal now? Is that what you're declaring?"

A ceiling mounted television sprang to life, cutting the swamp gloom with green and peach. Laila stared at him, her image appearing on one monitor after another, to surround him as much as the lowlives were. "Officer E11107 Blackstone, please put down your weapon and surrender yourself to security. Your actions have resulted in loss of life for a Gaia Corporation employee while on private property. You have violated your warrant and performed an illegal search of company premises. Security officers have been dispatched to apprehend you. Cooperate," the elf ordered.

Elliot licked his lips and stared down at the security officer. The man had crossed half the distance from the elevator to him, and now he was close enough that Elliot could see him. He had on a faceless mask, just like Brent, just like the cityboarder, just like the figures in Nguyen's game.

He put a bullet through the nearest monitor, right between Laila's eyes. The screen shattered, spraying sparks as plastic rained down into the bacterial digestion. "Get back," he bellowed. He swung the gun down to the thugs. "This is all being recorded. You have made clear and obvious threat to my life. I am acting in self-defense here and upholding the law of the land."

Some of them flinched. Not all of them. The leader just shook his masked head. "You killed one of ours, Jannis," he said.

Metal banged behind him. Someone had stepped onto a catwalk. Elliot spun, leveling the gun at them, and they froze. "I said get back."

Laila spoke in chorus, using every television's speaker system at once in a discordant echo. "Officer, surrender yourself. Proper arbitration requires you to be detained and investigative teams from both Gaia and from the Military Police to review the available data."

"Don't give me that shit," he snarled, swinging the other way as someone else tried to creep closer. That one had kicked a bucket, knocking the plastic tub of cleaning agent across the floor. "You think I don't know how that works? Indefinite stays in private prison cells don't interest me, not when you'll shut out and buy off any investigation." Someone else moved again; a half step into the light. "Stay back. I will shoot the next one of you that gets closer."

"Officer Elliot Blackstone," Laila said. The behavior of the construct changed. The movement of her arms became fluid and her expressions grew complex. She tapped a finger to her chin and frowned. "That's not your real first name, is it?"

Someone is sock puppeting.

"What's it to you? I've got four more bullets in this gun. I'm sure you could take me down if you wanted to, but the first one of you to charge is eating lead. Think hard fuckers, is your job worth your life to you?"

Laila laughed, a haughty chuckle where she feigned to cover her mouth with a hand. "Job? What are you talking about, you fossil? Here, Gaia Corp is a family. Our valued employees are in their homes, defending their livelihood and their brothers from an intruder. You're not fighting twelve people right now, you're fighting one mob with twelve bodies."

Twelve bodies and no faces... well, one face.

"You are a curious one though, aren't you, Elliot? If that's the name you want to be called by. Not many police officers come down to the ground floor, and yet you practically live here. What's more, you've got black spots on your public record," Laila said. "Redactions. Omissions. Things you would hope would stay hidden..."

Bile welled up in his throat. He stared at the nearest display of the elven sock puppet. "Is that how you're trying to threaten me now?"

"Something like that," the avatar said with a grin.

Pain exploded across Elliot's temple. His vision knocked away and then he realized he was falling.

Something hit me?

He hit the ground like a starting pistol and the twelve thugs sprinted at him. Elliot rolled, throwing up his gun to the air. The barrel swung. The man he aimed at threw himself to the ground, sliding to a stop a few meters away. Other footsteps pounded through the walkway.

Elliot spun. He was just in time to see a galvanized steel pipe fling through the air at him. He rolled, feeling it slam into his shoulder. Then off he went from the side. Half his body caught one of the algae sheets and the whole thing sprayed across him. The wet sheet of plastic was stiff though, which was good. He would have died if it hadn't been interposed between him and the officer's sledge hammer.

The blow cracked against the plastic, splitting it over Elliot's chest. His breath blew out of him, but up came his gun. A third gunshot exploded inside the tower. Blood squirted across him as the masked security officer howled. He wasn't dead though. The bullet had only hit him in the shoulder. The only thing it did was make him drop the sledge.

Elliot rolled and crawled on his belly beneath the nearest array of sewage treatment. Leaked and spilled filth soaked through his buttoned shirt and through his undershirt. It made his clothes cling like an ensnaring net, but he rolled out on the opposite side.

He was just in time to get a foot up and drive it into the mask of a lunging thug. The man grunted, and Elliot felt the mask twist. It only bought him a moment. The detective sprang up as the thug fit the mask back to his face. With only three shots left in his gun though, he didn't fire. He turned and ran.

"Catch him!" the security officer bellowed, and all the others scrambled to encircle him anew. Lights overhead flickered like a nightclub to keep each of them in darkness while spotlighting him.

Up. Need to get up to get help.

He went for the freight elevator. The bullet slowed the security officer down like an anchor, but it wasn't a free escape. Another faceless grunt vaulted over some piping and landed just between him and the elevator entrance. He hefted a monkey wrench in one sinewy arm.

Elliot shot him in the gut.

The wrench hit the ground with a bang, and the man doubled over to die with the softest thud.

Two left...

He jumped into the elevator and jammed the door close button, then the highest floor number he could spot. The rusted gate slid shut like it had to grind through broken glass.

"Go, go, get to the next floor and stop it." Two of the security officer's underlings threw themselves at the gate like rabid dogs, bouncing off the metal mesh fruitlessly. The cables groaned as slack stretched taut, but then the lift came free of the holds and carried him up.

Panic surged in him for a moment. He spun, and caught sight of the camera drone beside him. Breath surged out of him and his shoulders slumped. Then out came his phone. He dialed EVE and began speaking before he even got a response. "Officer in distress, repeat, officer in distress. I'm in Gaia Plantation One and under assault by twelve masked individuals. Backup requested immediately."

The elevator bounced to a stop, falling into new holding locks on the tenth floor. He had pressed the button for the fortieth floor, but the gates began opening anyways.

Elliot gulped and brought up his gun. Only a busy signal came back through his phone and he put it back in his pocket as he stared into the darkness of the tenth floor. Not a single shadow moved; no sign of anyone who had called for the elevator.

Why aren't the grow lights on?

The metal nozzle of a hose poked around the side before he could hit the door close button. He took aim, but there was no body. Water blasted out of it, hammering him in the face with a blinding torrent. It tasted worse than salt. Wet and cold, he threw up a hand to shield himself.

Something circular jammed into his chest and slammed him up against the far wall. Two different men screamed and charged him when the water stopped. Pinned to the wall, he tried to roll out from whatever had struck him—plastic piping. It caught one of his buttons and ripped his shirt before they descended on him like chimpanzees.

He blasted his sidearm and the bullet ricocheted off the support pillar. Neither thug flinched in pain. Hands grabbed hold of his arms, legs, and clothes. With him in their grip, they sank around him and struck. Fists hammered down on him like hammers; breaking him down into bloody pulp. He cried out in pain and one had the bright idea to slam his fist against the wall till he dropped the gun. It went spinning away and then he was truly at their mercy. The only thing he could do was put up his arms to shield his head. The pain went numb, one diffuse shock across his entire body.

The wounded security officer marched over. "Enough. Get out of my way."

Grovelling to their alpha, the two animals shrank away from Elliot and he got a glimpse of the man. He stood with the detective's pistol in one hand, silhouetted by an even larger display of Laila.

"To protect company privacy, all wireless communication is strictly prohibited," she said with a smile.

Elliot sighed and closed his eyes. His call hadn't gone through. He was out of options, so he put up his hands.

He was only at the man's mercy for a moment though. The tower rocked with an explosion. All of the thugs jumped and braced themselves. They spun as fire plumed on the far wall. Spotlights quickly replaced the momentary inferno. Shafts of light speared through the plantation, cutting shadows across the walls. The intruding thing didn't need to introduce itself.

One of the thugs screamed, "SWATBOT!"

Oh thank God.

11

SWATBOT

2140/09/06

"Officer in distress," the armored drone announced, the speaker booming through the entire city block. "This is Bastion Police Department Armored Response Unit Three. Set down all weapons. This is an order."

Elliot could finally laugh as the metal beast crawled through the gaping wound of a breaching charge. The ARU moved like a spider atop eight legs. Magnetic feet clasped onto floors, ceilings, pillars, walkways; anything with iron to it. The chassis in the middle drifted through the air seamlessly, swinging spotlights like seeking eyes.

The thugs screamed and scattered, turning their backs to the ARU as a fleet of reconnaissance drones swarmed inside. The smaller devices flew like harrying wasps, painting each in light and squawking orders to submit.

"It's a robot," the security officer bellowed. "Just put your fucking weapons down and you won't get shot."

Elliot chuckled. He could feel the trickles of heat—blood—down his face. "You sure about that? You're still holding a gun."

The thug spun and pointed the revolver at Elliot's forehead. There was one bullet left. Cold light blasted across his shoulders and he flinched. "Bastard," the thug said in a growl. Then he chucked the gun across the room. One of the recon drones snatched it out of the air and went bobbing away with it.

"This is ARU-3, put your hands up and get on your knees," the machine ordered as it crawled towards the two of them. The chassis of weapons hung beneath the head, a bulbous thing of lights and sensors that swiveled and twisted as it switched between various electromagnetic spectrums. At the moment, a belt-fed impact munition cannon pointed at the security officer's head.

The thug put up his hands, and for good measure so did Elliot. That mollified the steel beast. The security officer didn't take his face mask off, but he did get on his knees and face the machine.

A warning siren beeped.

The blood drained from Elliot's face.

"Warning, elevated biometrics indicate either use of controlled substance NZ-17, or possible infection of NZ pathogen. As per Congressional Order Seven, immediate confinement is required. Resistance will be met with lethal force. Additional ARU drones are being dispatched for your apprehension. Please cooperate."

Everyone in the room heard the cycling of metal and chains, the jangle of bullets. The non-lethal cannon beneath the ARU's chassis vanished inside and the grim barrel of a rifle emerged.

CZAR? They were tripping on CZAR in the fucking food supply chain?

"Run you idiots," the security officer screamed. He roared until the muscles in his neck bulged and his arms shook.

"Your cooperation is necessary," the ARU announced. "Fleeing arrest will be met with lethal force."

"Objection!" Laila shouted. "As per Congressional Order Seven, Amendment Three, you are required to have all analyses checked by human eyes before action."

The ARU froze, staring at one of the fleeing thugs as the recon drone gave chase. EVE's voice emanated from its speakers. "Amendment Twelve says that my judgment qualifies for Amendment Three's protections." The ARU began tracking again.

Laila's eyes had opened wide, to the very limit of the avatar's expressions. "Then you are in violation of Gaia Corporation private property. This is trespassing. Your right to action is limited strictly to the officer in distress." Again, the ARU froze.

The one to answer her objection was none other than Chief Alissa Cinder. His boss strolled in through the wreckage her toy had made and announced, "Enough with the legal jargon already. ARU, I am authorizing anti-material rounds. Take out these CZARheads."

Again, the gun beneath the robot cycled into the chassis, and another emerged. Aiming servos swung the barrel with pinpoint accuracy. The concussion of gunpowder was louder than the breaching charge. Ringing filled Elliot's ears. The bullet ripped through the floor, then the floor beneath that, and then someone screamed. Elliot had no doubt someone's brain had just been turned to red paint for the walls.

Then it aimed and shot again, and again, and again.

Laila could only stare. The display screen was large enough that Elliot saw her pupils twitching back and forth, reading something. Then the avatar's expression reset. The whole body recentered and regained the doll-like appearance that had been on it when Elliot first arrived at the tower.

I guess the puppeteer is gone...

Cinder came walking over to them, and Elliot struggled back to his feet. The swelling had begun, and he could feel his left brow trying to blind him. "Disgusting place," she said. Her face colored yellow from the guttering flame of a lighter. She inhaled, turning the tip of her cigar into orange embers. The smell of burnt tobacco snuffed out the stench of detritus. "You look like shit, Blackstone," she said.

The Chief of the Missou Police Department looked more like a soldier of fortune out of the South China Sea than a direct report to one of the most powerful men in the world. But then, Commander Ike had a lot of underlings, and the police needed someone willing and able to fight. She also looked like she had leapt out of bed to arrive in time.

Why the hell did she come in person though?

Her hair was an uncontrolled mess down her back and in her face. She had to brush it back every time she spoke, but it fell back in place as soon as she let go. As far as her misbuttoned shirt went, the security officer was surely thankful the mask hid his eyes. She still booted him in the chest before addressing him.

The thug crashed into the freight elevator, the bang of metal almost covered the sound of cocking her hammer back. "What the hell? You already got tagged? No wonder you were so pissed off," she said, pointing her own revolver at the bullet wound Elliot had put in him.

"This is brutality. You can't do this," he cried out, squirming away from her. Within the confines of the elevator, there was nowhere to go. Cinder blocked the entrance.

She laughed. "Really? You got any evidence of it? Because I've got tons of evidence that Gaia is illegally screening emergency calls. And who knows what I'll find now that I'm here pursuant to an active engagement. I dare say everything I set my eyes on would be admissible in court. Please, charge me with it. Make my day."

The security officer kept his mouth shut and his hands up. He barely even breathed.

"Chief Cinder," Laila said, the cadence of her words different than a moment before. "We thank the Bastion Police Department for their prompt intervention in this unfortunate event. It seems four of our employees were, unbeknownst to us, using CZAR and this led to a violent escalation. We thank you for bringing peace back to our establishment. It does however seem that things are at an end. If you need assistance getting Officer Blackstone to the hospital, our staff would be happy to help."

Someone else. Must be a lawyer.

Cinder's gaze switched back to Elliot and puffed on her cigar. "Can you walk?"

Elliot stood up. There was a cramp in his thigh and his knees were so bruised and swollen he was thinking he might have to cut his pants off that night. "I can walk."

Cinder whistled and the recon drones fell in line behind her. The moment she holstered her sidearm, the security officer scrambled to his feet and bolted. "Coward. I swear, nobody has any balls in this city."

"What are you doing here?" Elliot asked. One of his hands had gone to his side. The whole thing was tender, and he saw a brace in his future.

"Huh? Isn't it obvious?"

There is literally no way it was to help me.

Cinder pulled the cigar from her mouth and said, "Gaia lobbied to cut our budget. You think I'd pass up on a chance to kick their shit in? I don't let people fuck with me, Blackstone. You know that."

There it is.

The ARU fell in behind them once they got close to the gaping wall, and the whole mechanized troupe exited with them. Half a dozen other police officers mingled about on bridges and walkways. They had masks on too; bullet proof visors. He knew that if he got up to any of them, he could see their badge and likely could figure out who they were just by their stature and bearing. In the neon gloom though, they may as well have been machines.

He shook the thought out of his head. "So can I get a doctor before I get disciplined?"

Cinder laughed. "Good to see you still have your head on your shoulders. The problem is, we don't actually have a rule against following up on warrants in places like this. No one else on the force would need to be told this was a bad idea."

Elliot swallowed the knot that formed in his throat. The two of them were beside a train line. They weren't at a normal boarding station, but an emergency access bridge for city workers. The single car train sat with doors open for them, and once aboard it would just be the two of them. "Well, you know... I was following up to get some info for EVE for that bug report you wanted. For the 314 case? I had some time after my shift working the cityboarder junction like you asked me to."

"Oh, is that what it is? The 314 case I told you was internal only? Is that what this was? An internal investigation? Or did you just felt a burning need to stick your dick in an anthill?" Cinder asked, and gave him a shove toward the train. "Why don't you tell me all about it?"

For a moment, he could hear outside the tower. Dozens of people had gathered down on the ground, lit by phones and cigarettes as they recorded the police and shouted up at them. "Fuck you Jannis." "Get the fuck out of here, thugs!" "Go kill yourselves, not us."

Elliot and Cinder stood atop the bridge to the train, one wrong step from falling on the pitchforks below. The mob was inflamed with the knowledge that everything they thought about the police department had been proven right and all because Elliot had gone in to try and help.

The door slid shut behind them, and the train began to creep away. Elliot collapsed into a seat, legs spread out and arms limp in his lap. He couldn't bring himself to lift his head to look at his boss.

Cinder sat quietly as the train carried them away, but when Elliot didn't speak up, she said, "You're just one man, Blackstone. You might change one life here or there, but you're not going to change the city. The city doesn't care who you are or what you've done. The city won't ever know who the hell you are."

"What I'm doing is the right thing to do. No one ever cares about that."

"Don't let it get to you."

"Someone tampered with EVE's records. If there's an exploit, we'd never be able to track down the perp without figuring this out. The problem is the only guy I know of who could tell us... is the dead guy."

"Oh? And how is that supposed to help us? He's dead."

Elliot shrugged. "Well... I think he recorded it and put it in the video game he was developing. It's just that, the data is all encrypted, so I don't know how to get to it."

12

The Doll House

2140/09/06

"Ama-... Luck-E, you awake? Hello?"

The sterile glow of his kitchen light illuminated abandoned food on the table. Remnants of a microwave stir-fry, the brown sauce congealed and cracked like blood. Two open cans of beer sat beside the unwashed dish. That was the only sign of his absent wife.

Elliot shuffled inside. The doctors had strapped his chest into a brace to help the swelling in his side. It made him stand like he had a rod welded to his spine. The knots in his legs protested.

"Bastard's blood, you look like shit," his wife said from the doorway to their bedroom.

His mouth gaped open. "Lost a fight," he said. He had to grab the back of a chair for support. Her furrowed gaze made the stitches across his temple itch. Scratching them did nothing productive.

"Why didn't you shoot them? That bitch of a chief gives you a gun, doesn't she?" Amara asked as he pulled a seat out for himself and collapsed into it.

"I did." He picked up one of the cans and rattled it. "Got any more?"

His wife sneered at him. "It's like nine in the morning."

"So? It's never stopped you before, has it?"

"Aren't you on painkillers?"

"Oh, right," he said, and set the can back down. He sank in the seat, letting the back dig into his shoulders and hold him up. "I'm gunna be home for the next few days. Sort of administrative leave. Got in a shit-show with Gaia. The lawyers are going to hash things out. Cinder wants me out of sight," he said.

As though his words had summoned her, he felt his phone vibrate in his pocket. Cinder had messaged him. "If you want authorized over-time, I could use a warm body down at The Doll House at R7G13."

The strip club? Am I hired muscle now?

He didn't respond to the message, just sat it down on the table. "I was thinking maybe I could borrow your uplink and I could get some gaming pointers from you."

Amara snorted and walked over to the fridge. "I thought you hated gaming?" She got herself a beer and cracked it open.

Elliot licked his lips. "I do. But well, I have some motivation to try it at the moment."

She drank half the beer and shrugged. "Well, it's a good thing games can be played solo. I don't have any free time right now. The whole economy in B:GONE just fell apart because of a bug. If I don't snag something ridiculous in the auction, I won't have any content worth watching this week, so that's going to keep me busy all day."

You've got to be kidding me.

"Again?" he asked. He didn't even have the will to lift a muscle.

She shrugged at him. "What do you mean?"

"What do I mean?" he parroted back at her. "Amara-"

"Don't call me that!" she snapped at him.

"Luck-E, there is always some kind of event. Haven't you realized? There is always something going on. There is always some piece of en-tertainment that if you wait you can't get, but hey look at that, the next day there's something else that you can't wait to get. There is always something."

She scoffed and rolled her eyes. "That is not true. There are tons of dead days."

"Maybe in your particular opinion," he snapped at her. "I'm not say-ing everything is a fucking hit with every single player, but I am saying that even if you miss one thing there will be another, and another, and another. That's the business they're in. Stringing you along and taking your time."

"That's why it's fun. Not that you would understand. I haven't seen you do a single fun thing in years," she said, marching over to him.

He had enough anger to push himself back to his feet. "You haven't seen me do a single thing in years, fun or not. You have been completely consumed by that damn game."

Amara jabbed her finger into his chest, right into one of the straps for his rib brace. "Shows what you know. I've only been playing B:GONE for six months."

Elliot's lips curled into a snarl. "And before that was Zero-G, and before that was Embrace The Blood, and before that was Bonbon Saga. You think I don't know these things? Do you think that changes the point in the slightest? How many times have we had this argument and you still never listen to me."

She listened to that, just not the part he wanted her to hear.

Elliot found himself effectively tossed out again, unable to stand being with her any longer that day. He didn't even have the warm solace of the midday sun as he limped down the walkways around his house. His mind was a mess, a jumble of memories and heated fugue.

He walked right past Peasant Food without it even tickling his nose. Afterwards, he had a phantom of a memory that the waitress—the one who had put a blanket over him when he collapsed—had called out to him. It simmered to the top like rendered fat on top of a boil, but by the time it congealed, he had put too much distance between him and her. He was on a train flying between the towers, down to the depths of the city, and the train he was on didn't go the other way.

Going back would have been the direction of his fuming wife.

It was the plastic embrace of The Doll House that welcomed him. Not that any of the girls were plastic beyond the animal masks they all wore. Unrestrained flesh awaited his gaze wherever he looked, each with a coy mask that showed no other emotion.

"Officer, so good to see you." The words of the proprietor were like petroleum. Elliot knew the man. The strip club was merely one of a hundred properties he owned and operated. It let him bounce employees around as rewards and punishments. The well performing waitresses had the option of working his coffee cafes on the seventieth floor. The line chefs that showed up late or on slightly too many drugs, they ended up doing dish pit at a buffet. Mr. Mink also happened to be one of the chief lobbyists for the police department.

"A pleasure to be here as your hired muscle, Mr. Mink," Elliot said as one of the waitresses handed him a double whiskey on ice.

The landlord slapped his hands on his belly and laughed. He licked his lips as he watched Elliot sample the liquor, and waved him in. The two of them walked into the club, a mere few steps changing the entire color of the world. "You don't need to be so dour about it. I know this isn't conventional work for you, Mr. ..."

"Blackstone, or Elliot if you prefer."

Mr. Mink grinned. Despite all the dental prowess in the world, he was still missing several teeth. He hadn't even elected to replace them with gold. "Blackstone, I like that. That's a good name. Stone. It's strong, unmoving. I might use something like that the next time I need to give a bouncer a fake name, eh?"

"Do whatever you like."

"I do, and I will. Welcome to my paradise."

The Doll House opened up before them. The privilege of being with the owner was getting to skip the line, the coat check, and every scanner. He didn't have to explain the pistol in the back of his belt. They simply walked down the suede carpeted steps and into the grand hall of the strip club. The main room was three stories tall without a wall or pillar to disturb it; a great void within the tower.

A dozen half-dressed dancers flaunted from stage to stage, gyrating to the thump of EDM. A hundred people sat watching, filling the booths and clumped up seats. Some of them tossed tokens up to the girls dancing. The whole place was like an arcade; toss a coin in, get a girl to walk over and dance. The tokens weren't cheap though. Elliot knew that each of them was nearly a hundred credits. The place drank in money and in exchange, let the patrons indulge.

"Why the masks?"

"The masks?" Mr. Mink asked, slowing as the two of them ascended a narrow staircase in the back. "Privacy."

Every dancer had some kind of plastic facade. There were bunnies and foxes, dogs and cats. The attire only went as far as the chin. Everything from the neck down was bare skin.

"For the dancers?"

Mr. Mink laughed again and led him to one of the overhanging balconies on the third floor. It gave a wide view, but was in full sight of everyone below too. "For the dancers, yeah. Some of the girls are nervous about doing in the flesh the things they sell in digital for spare change. But it's also for the clients, you see? They don't want a girl, they want a body in front of them."

Elliot sat down at the table provided. There was already another whiskey on the rocks for him, waiting. The ice balls had cut the liquor more than he would have liked, but he sipped it anyways. "So, I just sit here and be seen? That's all I have to do to play my role here?"

Mr. Mink smiled and held his hands out. "Pretty easy, isn't it? If a fight breaks out or something, just uh, send up that little camera thingy you've got to get it all recorded. I've got some boys able and willing to deal with drunks."

"And if there's more than drunks?"

"There won't be. Please, Officer Blackstone, enjoy yourself."

The landlord left him there like a scarecrow. Any drink he ordered was on the house. His eyes had an all he could eat buffet of flesh. It saturated his brain until his thoughts had to squeeze through tar to be heard. The base, instinctual pleasure of the establishment wasn't so much a thought as a heat in the recessed, atrophied depths of his brain. Even the food, actual filet mignon that Mr. Mink had procured in exchange for his presence, dragged him deeper into the release of pleasure.

A girl in a cat mask walked over when they saw him stirring a chunk of meat through the remnants of powder-made mashed potatoes. "How's your evening going, Blackstone?"

"The same way my life is going; horrible," he said. "But who cares about the struggles of a jannis?"

The girl was young and attractive, her body fit with muscle but not lacking in fat. The mask covered everything from her chin to her hairline, and that sprouted out in neon green with twin braids that rested across her chest like clever censorship. When he glanced, she had a matching tail that stuck out from her latex shorts and bounced around with some internal mechanism.

She leaned in, her breasts hanging off her chest right in front of him. Her hand touched his knee. Warm. Every finger small and yet pressed against him so firmly. "Do you want some company?" she asked as she put one knee up on the table to crawl closer to him.

"I could use some company."

"What kind of company do you like?" She got both legs up on the table and put both of her hands on his legs. The way she arched her back made the tail rise up behind her and flick from side to side. He should have been able to smell her breath, the hint of her perfume.

He could only smell the stench of his own breath wafted back at him, repelled by the mask between them.

"The kind of company I like?"

She put a hand on his shoulder. He heard her breath as she drew closer. Her weight pressed him back into his chair. He couldn't take his gaze off the black slits that obscured her eyes. The circus of music, lights, and flesh beneath vanished from his mind.

"Is a complicated girl, one with all the stats about the War Games jammed into her brain by her asshole father, and big dreams about making it big as a video game streamer."

The cat girl laughed and straightened up. Both her hands found their way to his shoulders. Her fingers interlaced together behind his neck as she crawled off the table. The fit of her legs between the arms of the chair and Elliot's own was tight, but the soft embrace of her thighs was warm. "Please, don't get me started on the War Games. I'm contractually obligated to know all the latest talking points."

Elliot put his hands on the girl's legs. She didn't balk. His fingers felt the edge of her latex shorts; shockingly cold compared to her skin. "I always hated the War Games anyways."

"So, video games then?" the cat girl asked as she began to shake her hips from side to side. Her tail bounced like a hypnotist's coin.

Elliot laughed. "I hate those too."

The cat girl cocked her head at him. "You're not exactly making this easy, Mr. Blackstone. Do you have to unload about your work maybe? Is your boss a fat asshole who treats you like property?"

Elliot laughed as his hands slid down to the girl's knees. It hurt inside his chest, and not just his broken bones. "No, no Cinder isn't fat," he mumbled, and reached around her to get his whiskey. He didn't sip, he drank it; gulping the burning drink down.

It just made his stomach feel more twisted up.

"Sorry," the dancer said. "I must be projecting about my own boss."

"Did you ever think that Mink wasn't a very good boss?"

"Every day. So this company that you like. Does she have a name? Or have you only dreampt her up?"

"Her name is-" He stopped. The words tangled on his tongue, and he said, "She's my wife."

"And you're here... because? Your job said so?"

"Because we're closer than ever to divorce."

The dancer stopped, froze solid with her hip almost hanging her ass cheek off the side of the chair. "Well, I don't know how to break this to you, but this is more of a post-divorce establishment. Didn't the naked titties clue you in that I'm not a licensed therapist?"

Elliot laughed, but he was staring off, at the edge of the table he could see under the girl's arm. "The therapist didn't help anyways," he said. When he felt water in his eyes, he knocked back the last of his whiskey and wiped his face off. "You know." He sniffed hard and straightened up. "A man died last week, and nobody even noticed. Not his friends, not his family, his landlady, no one. Can you believe that?"

It was just me. I'm the only one in the whole city who cares, and nobody cares that I care.

She shrugged. "That happens every hour, doesn't it?"

"Not even EVE knew."

Silence dragged between them as she processed. "That's not possible. What did he do? Live his entire life with a mask on after being born in a shadow?"

"Masks? Like those ones with the holographic hole?"

The cat girl laughed. "Yeah, something like those void masks."

"Is that what they call them?"

She paused, and he had the impression she was smiling behind the mask. "They're new. I'm not even sure that's the name they're being sold under, but it's what people know them as."

"Any chance you know where I can get one?"

"Secondhand usually."

And no one would sell to a jannis.

He sighed and sank back in his chair. "So what is it? A pyramid scheme?"

"Personal is what it is," she said, sitting back down on his lap. "It gives them a history that's more than, well... data in a spreadsheet, like your John Doe isn't, I guess."

I feel like puking.

"And what would you know about personal? You don't even show your face."

"I'm showing everything else, aren't I?" she asked, and flipped up one of her braids. Elliot considered their age gap. "Besides, this is just my side gig. I work human resources for a living. But that's beside the point. So you've got a murder you'd rather be investigating than placating Mr. Mink, right? Is that what you'd rather talk about?"

Elliot shook his head and looked away. "I'm not supposed to talk about active investigations. You know, we're not even supposed to talk to journalists, just in case something we say gets taken out of context and becomes a soundbite that a lobbying group can dredge up in front of congress. Don't you find that a little ridiculous?"

He found himself staring back at the girl, one hand gripping the arm of his chair.

"Sounds risk averse anyways. Someone at some point must have made a really big mistake, and you're still paying for it, right?"

He huffed, flaring his nostrils. "You'd think so, but no one ever has a specific example. It's... it's... like, generalized. People have this impression and because of that, then everything must be like that, because they have this impression, you know?"

He was working his hands through the air between them, trying to grasp onto the idea that he couldn't nail down with words.

"You mean like how everyone hates the police, despite having virtually no interactions with them?" Something in her voice had changed. The playfulness was gone, her coyness missing.

"Yes. People look at me and they don't see me, they don't see my badge, they see a uniform that they've only ever before seen on the news. I'm just a walking impression no matter what I do, and the moment I walk away, they forget everything I did."

"Mr. Blackstone... sir... do you need another drink?"

Elliot looked at the tumbler in his hand; nothing but ice melt. "No... no, what I need is a computer I can borrow, and an uplink. I'm going to go fucking kill a monster."

13

Sticks and Stones

2140/09/06

Elliot felt like everything he had ever learned in his life had been wiped away, made useless, by stomping around in [The Faceless Well].

What the hell do other people see in this crap?

All he needed was to know was why the developer had been deleted from the system and why he had indulged the lack of identity by wearing a mask. Getting the recordings the man had made in Steppe Up was as close to speaking with him as he could get, and that meant finding them in the game.

Elliot kept reminding himself of that as he wandered through the town of [The Faceless Well]. The monster-hiding well waited for him, like the center of the whole world, while he went looking for something like a quest explanation, a hidden treasure chest, a talkative non-player character.

He didn't get so much as an auditory chime to clue him in.

The first weapon he picked up, if it could be called that, was nothing but a hefty stick with a knot at one end. It felt like a proper cudgel in his hand, but there was stat block to explain its capabilities. The only thing that made it special was that he could actually pick it up at all.

The world looked real, but trampling through the grass left no impression. The rocks sat as firmly as iron in the ground. Even the flimsiest of wooden walls couldn't be budged; their physics had all been disabled.

He gave the improvised cudgel a few swings, knocking it against rocks and timber, feeling the weight. Just to be sure, he smashed in the head of one of the faceless mannequins that populated the simulated world. It worked well enough for an unmoving, unresisting target; but...

Can't kill a fucking squid with a bludgeon though, can I?

The sun overhead shone across the world from a static spot, no matter when he logged in or how much time he spent in it. Some simulations would tinker with the flow of time, but this one had frozen it entirely. It made gauging the passage of time a dull nightmare.

The cottage stolen from B:GONE was the strangest of them all. The inside was empty, not even with enough supports to hold up the roof. It looked like everything had been stolen from the insides. The whole building sat beside the road as nothing but a shell; a facade.

It was the building next to the cottage that seemed to finally have fruit for him. That was the smithy he had noticed before getting sucked in by the well. The structure was meandering and felt half complete. Where he expected walls, there were only a few columns an an overhanging awning of thatch. The stone furnace was the mightiest feature in it, sitting stouter in the middle than any bakery oven he could imagine. The heat of the coals radiated out and dried his skin as he approached; a delicate sensation to simulate.

Two mannequins stood in the smithy, toiling over shapes of iron. His gut told him one should have been the master, and the other the apprentice, but both figures seemed to be of an age.

They look like Nguyen's age.

Elliot took his time, inspecting the smithy like he would have inspected a crime scene. His familiarity with how a blacksmithy should have looked came up woefully short. There were barrels most of all, barrels of raw materials he could barely identify.

The witnesses, as they were, didn't complain when he pried one lid open after another. Coal, charcoal, oil, water, salt water, sand, bone, iron ore, and powders he couldn't guess at. Nothing felt out of place, nothing worth investigating until he spied the smithing hammer. It was a short thing with a heavy head of metal. He picked it up. He couldn't hold it upright. The handle was far too short to be used as a weapon.

"Does speaking work? Eh?" he asked, turning his gaze from one figure to the next.

Neither reacted.

What am I doing here?

He left the smithy and went around the town square one by one, sticking his head into buildings. There were barren cafes and locked houses. Tool shops and trade goods, mixed with grocers and a medieval pharmacy.

Then he forced open the door to a stone building that had iron bars for windows. Not a soul—mannequins anyways—was inside. The function of it was obvious at once to him; a guard house.

It's kind of like all the walls are missing though.

All the tools of the trade were on tracks across the walls, cluttering every side save the corner reserved for holding cells. The stench of ammonia and hay was blessedly missing from the simulation, but the foul staining had been included across the stone foundation. The mere thought of sleeping against those cold rocks made him shiver.

"This will do nicely," he said as he stepped behind some form of steward's desk and got to the weapon rack. He hefted up a polearm. The wooden handle fit in his hand well, the grain rough against his palms just like the entrenching tools from boot camp. The crescent moon edge felt sharp to his thumb, as sharp as the program could simulate through his neural uplink at least, and the point was like a spear.

He left the empty guardhouse and went back to the well. Once more, he knocked the bucket in and let it fall into the water. This time, he only gave it a few tugs, like knocking on the door, then stepped away.

"Come on, you fucking slimy bastard," he screamed, shaking his weapon in the virtual air.

The monster emerged a moment later, no hauling required. Elliot grasped the polearm in both hands, pointing the tip at the monster until enough of the tentacles had emerged that he dared to hack at one.

As though he were cleaving firewood to kindling, he slammed through the end of one of them. The metal chopped through flesh and bone, and bounced off the stone beneath. Blood squirted like from a flopping hose.

"Ha!" he shouted, watching the cyclopean head sway.

The monster hissed and slathered from its pointy mandibles. The other seven tentacles reared up at him, poised and appraising.

Elliot thrust the point at the main body. He didn't reach the torso of it. The tip impaled one of the tentacles and bit through sinewy muscle. Muscle that binded down on the metal and took hold.

Before he could jerk his hands back, the monster twisted and wrenched the tool from his grasp. He cursed, feeling the wood rip against his skin before popping free. Then he was defenseless again. For a single breath, he faced the monster of the well bare handed.

Then it ripped him apart and killed him.

Elliot's awareness burst back into reality with a thrash. The cat girl had to grab her drink away from the table when he kicked it, barely keeping the liquor from spilling across her lap. "No luck?"

Elliot slowed his breathing down and cleared his eyes. He had to slide the ENU—external neural uplink—back into place and he picked up his half finished can of beer. "It's a wily little bastard, I'll give it that," he said, and killed the drink. "Gunna feel good to fuck it up."

"Did you learn something?"

"Pertaining to the investigation? No. But I did get a weapon."

"I think you need a better weapon, or practice," she said and put her elbow up on the balcony railing.

"Both." He took a quick survey of the club. Nothing seemed different from when he went in, not from when he had arrived.

He jammed the power button to restart his connection to [The Faceless Well].

The monster killed him again.

He came out snarling and growling. His heart raced with adrenaline, and he punched the boot-up again.

The monster smashed his brains across the ground.

The dancer forced him to take a break after that, despite his efforts to hit the boot-up again. Knots were forming across his body from the imagined sensations. Sweat had matted his undershirt to his body and the stains were starting to show across his uniform. When she finally got it away from him, he sank in the chair. "I'm not very good at this, am I?"

The cat girl shrugged. "I mean, I wouldn't have been the one to say that aloud."

"Just think it?"

"That's the polite way to do it, isn't it? The masks help too. I don't even need to hide my disgust when some fat bastard rolls up with a thousand credit token to shove into my hands. The hand sweat, oh my God, the greasy hand sweat I have had to feel," she said. She recoiled from the table and had to shake the memory off.

Elliot shook his head and pulled the headset off. "I need to think up another strategy."

"Any guides available online?"

He scowled. "Guides? Like someone to come in and beat the game for me?"

The cat girl held her tongue for a moment, and said, "No, I mean an explanation of how to tackle it. Some literature. If you aren't one to play video games, then do you read or something?"

"I work," he said, and turned on the service light. "Everyone's always asking me about that anymore. I spend my time working. It's more engrossing than entertainment is."

She shrugged. "You just haven't found the right kind of entertainment."

"Maybe. But, that's beside the point. The victim never released the game, so how could there be a guide?" he said as one of the serving girls walked over to them. She was short, with mismatched tattoos covering most of her skin, but her curves jiggled in an eye-catching way as she moved.

While he was ordering, the cat girl said, "Well, I'd volunteer myself, but I'm not actually very good at games."

"You can't access the department server anyways," Elliot said after the waitress walked off to get him a rye whiskey and a caffeine pill.

"My advice," she continued, "would be to call up someone who's a savant at games and explain the situation. The right kind of gamer can probably just tell you how to do it from a brief explanation. Some people are just like that."

Amara would know. She wouldn't stay on the line long enough to tell me though.

"A shame there isn't some kind of division in the police department to deal with this kind of stuff. Special Games And Strategies or something," he said. He drummed his fingers on the ENU. The color of the club had changed. He couldn't put his finger on what had done it, whether the hue of the lights were different or if the prevailing fashion had changed over the hours.

"SGAS?"

He glanced back over at the cat girl. "I didn't say I was good at acronyms. They usually crowd source those anyways. The best ones come from asking a few thousand people for good ideas and hopefully one of them has a good idea."

She shrugged and turned up her hands. "So, no friends that are good at games?"

Elliot opened his mouth to answer, but as soon as he did, the waitress returned with his drink, and he paused. The moment it took for him to eat the caffeine pill and wash it down with whiskey was enough to connect some thoughts. "Actually, I might know someone with some time on their hands."

14

The Right Kind of Guidance

2140/09/06

Dom curtly responded to nearly two pages of text about [The Faceless Well] with a single sentence, "Go back to the smith and make a sword."

If the cat girl next to him hadn't talked him out of it, he would have called up the punk kid to chew his ear off and get a proper response, but deference to the boy's experience won out, and as night set over Bastion, Elliot returned to the blacksmith and picked up the forging hammer.

After so much time in the game, his senses had begun acclimating to the nuances, and he could feel the heat of the furnace once he was beside the mannequins. The mouth of the stone dome glowed from coal embers, and sticking out from it was a black iron tang. A half finished blade still cooked in the heat.

He used a hefty pair of tongs to pull the metal out and hold it before himself. "How the hell did he know this would be here?" The chunk of metal had the right shape, but no edge.

Elliot popped the top off a water barrel and quenched the steel. The metal hissed, boiled the water, and fractured straight through the middle. Half the blade sank through the barrel like his hopes sank in his chest, and then he heard the thunk of metal at the bottom.

"Son of a bitch."

Rather than admit what happened to anyone, he logged out and back in, resetting the simulation. He returned to the smithy, and chose another barrel to quench it. The oil was wrong too, but the salt water turned out to be right.

When he went to put on an edge, nothing he did to spin the wheel and press the steel would work. Sparks flew, the pumice grinded, but no progress was made.

Damn cleaver is too thick.

He reloaded, went back, and before quenching it, he picked up the hefty hammer and slammed the raw material. It ballooned, bent, and warped from one strike from the heavy hammer; completely destroying the shape.

"Son of a bitch."

This is why I hate puzzles.

Before reloading the simulation, he vented by chucking the hammer across the room. He aimed for the wall, but he didn't get the satisfaction of the crash.

The mannequin moved and snatched the hammer from the air. A moment later, it hunched over the anvil with it in hand.

Elliot sighed and reminded himself that Richard Nguyen's recordings were somewhere in the game and killing the monster was the best guess he had. So he reloaded the simulation. He went back to the smithy. He gave the mannequin the hammer and then handed it the raw weapon.

The artificial blacksmith pounded the steel into shape, working it flat and shaping a fuller. The entire process took only a few moments, and then ceased. Elliot took the shaped weapon and quenched it, then put on and edge with the grindstone.

As soon as he could grip the sword in his hand and see the edge, he left the smithy. He knew there was more to a proper sword, but he didn't need a crossguard or a pommel or anything else to stab a monster to death.

He shoved the bucket over the edge of the well. "Come on, get up here you bastard." It splashed into the water. The instant one of the tentacles crawled up from the depths, he attacked. The sword cleaved off the tip of the fishy appendage.

Out came another tendril, squeezing up as the corpulent body emerged. Elliot was ready for it, and cut that one too. Then the third and the fourth, forcing the monster to rise head first.

It hissed and roared, snapping mandibles as it looked for him.

"Over here," Elliot said, grabbing the sword with both of his hands and pointing the tip. When it turned to face him, he drove it forwards and lanced the monster through the eye.

A death screech exploded through the plaza as the monster reared back and thrashed. The sword was ripped from Elliot's hands, but dark blood sprayed like rain in every direction. The detective jumped away as the sea monster's head swung like a wrecking ball and finally crashed to the ground. A purple tongue lolled out and it exhaled.

"Are you dead?" he asked.

To answer, the monster slid down into the well. The tension that had kept it up at the top melted and it fell back to the water with a colossal splash. White foam plumed like a volcano and coated the courtyard, washing the monster blood away.

Elliot burst out laughing. It erupted from him, and he felt his whole body shake with every blast of exaltation. "Take that you tentacled fuck! And fuck you Nguyen. Screw you and your bullshit difficulty. I did it. I was fucking good enough and I don't even play video games."

He ran back over to the well, and found a ladder leading down that hadn't been there before. The depths were still dark, but he couldn't see the monster corpse either.

His manifesto rant had better be down there.

The moment he grabbed onto the edge of the well and swung a foot over to climb down, someone ripped the ENU off his head and shoved him back into The Doll House. It felt like someone had changed the channel of the television on him, a forced switchover of every sensory input. The reality of the Doll House, that he had put himself in, dragged him back down into the naked filth of instinct and desire.

Why the hell am I here?

"Officer, get up," Mr. Mink shouted.

The first thing he comprehended was that the landlord was spitting as he spoke, a spray of mouth filth that misted Elliot's entire front. Then he heard the shouting. "Bastard's blood," he growled. He tried to rise, but his head throbbed like a hangover was setting in. "What? What's happening?"

Mr. Mink answered him, but the words sounded like a mumble in the music. While he had been out, the sound track had gotten louder and grungier. More of the notes were thumps and noise. The bass line more guttural to break through a haze of alcohol and keep the masses in sync. The masses were shouting though.

"Hooligans are attacking. They tazed my security."

The detective groaned and pushed himself standing. His body gave a few pangs of protest, bruises and fractures waking up the same time he did. The alcohol had dulled the pain, not removed it. He grimaced, but he surveyed the club like a roused eagle nonetheless.

Half a dozen kids had broken through the doors and run havoc . Most of them wielded cans of spray paint like pepper spray. The chemical difference wasn't notably different as far as people's eyes were concerned either. The kids couldn't have caused more panic if they had been spraying fire into the crowds while they cackled to one another, laughing about scores and points for who they managed to tag with the paint.

The mere thought of getting the wrong corporation's color on their outfit made the club patrons shriek and flee. They scattered away and climbed over one another, thus giving the kids all the room they needed.

One of them, a ringleader of sorts, went after the girl on the main stage. They were two and a half stories down, so Elliot could only watch as the dancer was chased down. The ringleader didn't beat her or anything, but he did grab hold of her by the wrist and stop her. The six inch heels she had been wearing may as well have been ankle cuffs. She fell on her ass at his feet and was at his mercy when he ripped off her mask.

He took a picture of her face, and the data transferred to all of his partners. The masks they had been wearing flashed, and then each of them was wearing the girl's face in front of their own. They hooted and hollered and shoved their new look into the faces of the club customers.

Laughter spread like a contagion.

The cat girl shook her head. "I'm getting out of here. They just killed her."

It's just one thing after another, isn't it? I guess Cinder at least had a reason to send me here. Fuck though; right when I was going to wrap up the Nguyen case.

"What are you doing?" Mr. Mink demanded. He threw up his hands as he spoke, gesturing at the railing. Despite his gesticulating, he never left the shadows, he didn't stand anywhere he could be seen. "Aren't you supposed to be the law and justice around here? Go put a stop to this. I can't run a business if I don't have employees."

Elliot hung his head until he could put on a smile. Then he turned back to the landlord and said, "Right away, Sir. The boys in blue have your back." The words were bitter in his mouth.

Mr. Mink looked like he held back spitting. "For the amount I spend on you, you'd better."

Bastard.

"Call it in to the station though, would you? I'll need extra hands to haul them all to jail," he said, and shoved off the railing to walk into the darkness of the third floor.

"Way ahead of you, Blackstone. Go do something already," the landlord hollered as he headed down the steps.

15

True Naming

2140/09/06

Elliot came hunting from the back. He strode through an eddy in the crowds. People shouted, music blared, and nobody had yet turned on the full lights. People still shoved past one another in the disco flashing of a dozen spotlights of different colors. They swung their arms overhead like they were swimming through the crowd.

Half the chaos wasn't even related to the break-in. He passed people diving over bar counters to steal liquor bottles, and heard the shattering of glass. He saw the bartenders only from the corner of his eyes. He didn't need to watch them beat the would-be thieves over the head. He could hear the thumps and cracks easily enough. What he needed to see was the root cause.

The first one was easy enough to find. He heard the squeaky cackle of late puberty and veered right at him. "Me? Join the military?" the kid was saying. "Oh no, no you have me misread, my good sir. You see, I am an intellectual and my place in society is much higher; the upper echelons of academia in fact. You know, I told that to the draft recruiter and you know what he said to me? I'll tell you what he said to me. He said, 'Son, you're too Goddamned poor to go to college without serving your country first.' Well, I didn't very much like the idea of killing stragglers for the government so-"

Elliot grabbed the kid by the wrist; handcuff first. The steel ratcheted shut, clicking all the way to the smallest setting to fit his bony limb. The hooligan shouted as he was spun around, and Elliot saw him head on. The clothes looked like bargain bin sweats. Elliot snarled. It was the subsidized clothing kids ended up in when they were both homeless and too incompetent for the draft.

The mask the kid was wearing was a thin, digital display with some black cloth to hide his actual face. The terrified face of the dancer covered the hooligan's, along with data about her; name, address, occupation, schooling history, major usernames, the works.

"Oh fuck!" the kid shouted, but he couldn't pull free of Elliot's grasp. The detective snapped the other end of the handcuffs around a steel pipe overhead. Then he snatched the mask off his face.

The bespectacled kid shrank in on himself reflexively and tried to say something. He tried to, but all the words choked up in his trembling throat as he stood in front of Elliot.

"You're under arrest," the detective growled, jabbing the kid in the chest with a finger. "Smile for the camera," he said, pointing at the drone over his shoulder. Then he turned on the woman the kid had been speaking to. She was fully dressed, unlike the employees, and seemed nonplussed by his presence. He leaned in and his lips curled back from his teeth as he asked, "What the Hell is wrong with you?"

"What?" she asked. "I just helped you arrest him, didn't I? Is it a crime to be calm?"

"No, I suppose it's not a crime; but, maybe it should be."

She sucked on her drink, slurping bubbles through her straw as she looked him up and down. "Shouldn't someone like you have a more personable partner or something? One to do the people talking thing that you're clearly no good at? Because I'd rather speak to the other cop."

"I am the friendly cop," Elliot said, and gave the kid a quick glare to drive out the thought of escaping from his mind. Then, he went for the ringleader. Micro-gangs were like mushrooms; they always sprouted back up in the dark. The other four running mayhem were the ones doing the property damage, but it was the ringleader that had nucleated them to action. He was the head of the snake.

The layout of the club, now that he was in the main pit with most of the people, reminded him of an old sporting arena. Instead of a court that all the rising booths faced, it was a stage with half a dozen poles and more tip tokens covered the floor than losing lotto tickets in a liquor store.

All eyes surrounded him and the ringleader's spectacle.

"Claire Elleson," The ringleader announced, amplifying his voice throughout the club with a pocket speaker. It reflexively drew attention back to him; people wanted to know whether he was calling someone out or making an announcement. They were his audience as much as they were his victims, and he went on to toss red meat to them. "She is in fact twenty-nine years old and she does not just work here on the weekends like she may have told you. She works five nights a week, eight hour shifts, just split between The Doll House and Gold Academy on the other side of Bastion. Both a draft flunkee as well as a college drop out, but doing some quick math here, thanks to the kind patronage of all you people out here to facilitate it, she makes fifty-thousand credits... per month."

The words blindsided Elliot. He nearly stumbled on the steps as he reconciled the facts.

She makes more in two months than my entire salary.

The girl trembled, fear filling her eyes. The hooligans had her surrounded with her own face looking back at her. Beyond them were hundreds of people wondering how she was worth that kind of money. The people pulled away from her, sympathy shifting to disgust.

"That's a lie!"

The ringleader shook his head. "Tell that to her apartment on the forty-second floor. I wish I lived up there. It seems to me that selling the idea of intimacy is just about the most lucrative thing a girl can do nowadays. She doesn't even need to whore herself out physically, she's doing it emotionally and is oh so successful at it."

"Shut your jabbering," Elliot ordered, and stepped up on stage. He brandished his badge in one hand. "You're under arrest for breaking and entering, assault with a deadly weapon, and whatever else the prosecutor can pin you with."

The ringleader looked over at him, dropped the microphone, and whipped out a spray can. Elliot flinched, lifting up his badge towards his face, but no blast of paint came. "Eat neural jamming!" the kid shouted, and pressed the button.

Elliot's brow pulled tight and he braced. The device squawked and crackled with electricity, but nothing else. The detective strode hard to the side, putting himself between the dancer and the ringleader.

When nothing happened to him, the kid shook the device a few times and jammed the button as fast as he could. He pointed it like a gun and when Elliot marched towards him, he shrank backwards.

"What the hell is this?" Elliot demanded, snatching the thing from the ringleader's hands, just as the dancer screamed behind him. He spun about to see her on her knees, covering her eyes with her hands. He fumbled the off switch. The moment it stopped, she puked.

Elliot frowned and looked the device over. Rather than a depression cap at the top, there were a couple buttons. The tube was just to obfuscate it.

What the hell is this? Who the fuck made something like this?

When he looked up, the ringleader was sprinting full speed away from him, vaulting over booths and toppling tables. He had ripped the mask from his face, though a balaclava still covered everything but his eyes.

"Stop that man," Elliot bellowed, and gave chase. Thankfully, someone did. The moment Elliot tried to run was the moment his body remembered he had just gotten the shit kicked out of him the night before, and all the liquor in the club wasn't enough to take that pain away. He could only stumble and wince, clutching at his rib brace while bruises spasmed.

It was the club security that caught the kid. The one who had been tazed had gotten back to his feet, and then planted one of his feet in the ringleader's chest. The size difference between the two was like a child and a giant. The ringleader went tumbling across the floor until he hit a booth and stopped. "That's called payback, bitch," the security guard said, scratching a burn mark on the side of his neck. Elliot at least assumed it was his neck; there didn't seem to be much distinction between head and shoulders on the security guard.

Elliot was able to get to the kid before he got back up, and drove a knee into the ringleader's back. "I suggest you start cooperating," he said, wrenching one arm and then the other behind the kid's back to handcuff him face down on the beer-slick floor. Then he tugged the balaclava off the kid's face to get a recording of it.

"Son of a bitch. You've gotta be fucking kidding me right now. They sent a jannis without an implant here?" the kid asked as he spat stray hair from his mouth and glared at him. "What kind of fucking person doesn't have a neural implant nowadays?"

Elliot looked again at the 'neural jammer'. "What can I say? Never got around to it. Who gave you something like this?"

"Fuck you. I'm not telling you anything. I didn't do anything wrong here."

The detective sighed and glanced around the room. "The paint alone cost probably a thousand credits worth of damage, and that's assuming you didn't get it in anyone's eyes. That's jail time you idiot. Now who gave you it?"

The kid spat on the ground.

Elliot pulled out his phone, accessed the facial recognition app, and scanned the kid's face. A moment later, EVE had everything. He read off, "Harold Cuther. Goes by Harry. You were rejected by the draft three months ago. Last official residence was with your mother at the community complex, but you were kicked out on your eighteenth. No permanent residence since, but you tend to sleep at Forgotten Books down by the river, because the owner lets you sleep in exchange for sorting their used collection. And now, soon to be resident in jail."

"Don't call me that, jannis," Harry demanded. "At least read that bullshit database correctly."

Elliot paused and reread the report on his phone. "GalahadTheMighty? You want me to use your Chivalry Arena username or something?"

GalahadTheMighty huffed and kept his mouth shut after that.

Elliot sighed. "If you've got a lawyer, I suggest you reach out to them," he said, and ran his hand through the hair on the back of GalahadTheMighty's head. He felt the scars. "And just so you know, if you try using your neural implant for anything other than that, EVE will detect it and you can be charged with resisting arrest."

The security guard walked over and glared at GalahadTheMighty, but Elliot didn't say anything about it. When the ogre of a guard offered to give him a hand, the detective didn't refuse and went to get the others.

The first kid he had cuffed was gone. The metal loops dangled uselessly from the pipe.

"Son of a bitch."

He couldn't spot any of the other attackers and after a moment, the music and lights all switched over like closing time had come a few hours early.

He headed back over to Claire and found her sobbing in a corner, smelling like vomit. "My life is ruined." Mascara streamed down her cheeks.

Maybe you shouldn't have been doing this then. What do you expect me to do about that?

"Worry about your future later. How's your health?" he asked, and knelt down beside her. Her shoulder was warm when he put his hand on it. "What happened? What did that neural jammer thing do?"

She wiped her snotty nose and waved him off. "It just messed with my ad-block. You'd puke too if you had to see everything Mink has in here."

"Glad I don't. Other officers will be here soon. We'll see what can be done about your privacy issue," he said, and stood back up. The woman at the bar had been right; he wasn't the best to talk to people like this, and he knew it.

"EVE," he said, pressing his phone to his ear as he walked back to the captured ringleader. "Get me Devson, would you? I need an expert opinion here."

"I'm sorry," the AI responded. "I cannot put you through to Devson right now. There appears to be some form of restriction on your communications, Officer."

He stopped.

"What the hell does that mean?" he asked.

EVE said, "I'm not entirely sure myself. The nature of the block has been obscured from my processing. It may be a general outage, a relay disruption between my ghosts, or you were blocked directly. It might be on his end. He's got a deadline coming up for his contract work with Dimeworks. I guess there are some things other than politics that can keep a sys-admin's attention."

He knows he would lose his job if he blocked me... right?

"Put me through to Cinder then."

"Chief Alissa can only be contacted by special means right now because she is directly piloting an ARU."

Crazy woman.

He sucked in breath and puffed up his chest till the rumbling of frustration quelled. "Who the hell can I contact then?"

After a pause, EVE said, "I could put you through to Mr. d'Angelo."

Elliot's eyes rolled. "I'll figure it out on my own. Other officers are already en route, right?"

"Correct," the AI said. "The QRS should arrive in less than ten minutes."

"I don't suppose I still have your attention?"
The call died on him and he scowled at his phone.
I guess this is too mundane for her.

16

Shot In The Dark

2140/09/06

"GalahadTheMighty, galahadthemighty, galahad the mighty. Do your friends really call you that? It's a mouthful of syllables, isn't it?"

The kid's cheeks darkened. "Most call me Galahad."

No way he got that name though.

"Still pretty long. Also, your friends didn't stick around much, did they?" Elliot said, dropping into the nearest seat. He looked around the club again; the hooligans were gone and the chaos subsided. The whole fiasco had ended in fifteen minutes.

"Why would they, jannis?" Galahad asked.

He shrugged. "If the city wills it, they'll be caught. Your friends don't call you Galahad either, do they? Let me guess; Gal? Gallium?"

"None of your business," Galahad said, turning his gaze to the floor. The scuffed plastic tiles weren't much to look at though.

Elliot nodded. "I'll go with Gal. Why'd you do this, Gal? Why did you think you'd get away with it?"

The kid's answer came in the form of a glance back towards the stage; back in the direction of the dancer.

Elliot sighed. "Well, it was your bad luck that I don't have any wet-ware I guess. You don't have to talk. You'll get brought into the station, and we'll start by having EVE run a full history on you. You just have to stay here until my backup arrives. Why don't you tell me something though. Was this for fun? Or is somebody paying you and your friends to run around and do their bidding in these masks?"

GalahadTheMighty glared at the ground and didn't answer.

"Come on, kid. You're young still. Don't you realize it'll be in your best interest to cooperate? You look like you're about to get drafted. Your whole life is going to change-"

"The hell do you know about that?" the kid screamed, his face red. "How would you know? Huh? You who made it in. Even a piece of shit, bottom of the totem pole cop like you still made it. What would you know about what it's like for us on the bottom of the city?"

Elliot shook his head. "More than you realize kid. I know what it's like to be hated by everyone around you, just because of who you are. I know what it's like to slave all day and make pennies. That Claire girl? I could retire on her income. You better believe I'm jealous of that. What I don't understand is why you'd go and make life worse for other people, just because you've had it hard."

The red faded from the kid's cheeks, but he kept his mouth gritted shut.

"Look, if you can help me out on another investigation, if you help me get the guy coordinating you, I can try to help you out. Think about that. The QRS will be here soon to haul you to jail. If you're going to squeal, I suggest you squeal before you get put in the group cell... What is taking the QRS so long though?"

The security guard grunted and pulled a chair over. He sat down next to Gal and folded his arms. "They're probably delayed trying to get all the runaways. I hate these kinds of raids."

Elliot shrugged and put his hands in his pockets as he rose. "If they're on foot, they'll get picked up. If they're crazy enough to use cityboards, they might slip free."

The security guard laughed. "I'd love to see some of you MPs trying to keep up on cityboards. I'd pay money to see it in fact. And I don't mean some robot, but, that's never gunna happen. The other cops are probably rounding them up right now, anyways."

The detective sighed. "The problem is every second that passes, the net has to get wider. It'll depend on when they get here."

"When?" the guard asked, his face squeezing together in a caricature of confusion. "They already here though. One of your friends is upstairs with Mr. Mink."

Elliot pulled his phone back out. He had no alert. "Are you sure? Did they tell you their name?" he asked.

The guard frowned and scratched the burn mark on his neck again. "What was it?" he mumbled. "Pretty sure he gave his badge number, but I was all foggy from the zap this one gave me." He nudged Gal in the shoulder with his boot. "A... it was A something."

A-rank? A-rank is only given to department chiefs.

The guard's eyes unfocused as he looked at something with his neural implant. "Ah, right, got it. It was A55013."

"His badge number was Asshole?" Elliot asked.

The guard laughed and grinned. "Yeah, I guess it is."

Elliot didn't laugh, he drew his revolver and started running. He stomped back up the stairs, pulling himself up with the railing and flying around bends. He didn't shout though, he kept his mouth shut until after he reached the top floor and took a look. It was dark and the patrons hadn't felt particularly threatened by spray paint two stories beneath them, so he had to scan the balconies twice.

Then he spotted the same blue jacket he wore. A man was halfway across the club, held up talking to one of the half-dressed serving girls. Mr. Mink was screaming at someone further beyond and hadn't met the so-called police officer yet.

Elliot pushed through the crowd, shoving people left and right to clear room. "Bastion PD, get out of my way, move, move!" he shouted, but he was one voice in a growing din. Mr. Mink saw the commotion and finished up his conversation. The landlord started walking his way, but also in the direction of the fake.

No, no, go the other way.

"Officer," Elliot barked, and the fake turned to face him. The man's expression changed in a flash from impatience to panic. Elliot thrust his badge into the air and used it to shove closer. "I am officer E11107, Missou department. Identify yourself," he ordered, omitting the pleasantries.

A few people saw his glare and knew well enough to get out of his way, especially when the fake didn't even turn back around to face him. It wasn't enough though. Elliot could barely move faster than a walk by the time he saw the fake reach into his jacket, and it wasn't the pocket where a badge should have been kept.

He fired.

Not at the fake; there were too many bystanders both in front and beyond him. He shot a light out overhead, adding a shatter of glass to the report of his gun. People screamed and threw themselves to the ground.

Well that's reckless discharge.

The fake didn't drop, he did flinch though. And in his hand was the grip of a pistol. He made eye contact with Elliot.

"Get down now!" Elliot took aim.

The fake bolted, straight at Mr. Mink.

Elliot fired once, putting a bullet in the fake, but not stopping him. He couldn't fire again, not without killing a bystander.

The landlord got the message loud and clear when he saw the look in the fake's eyes. Mr. Mink shrieked and stumbled back. Then he grabbed hold of one of his customers and shoved them between him and the assailant.

The next shot came from the fake, and ripped right through the customer's gut and through to Mr. Mink's chest. Both of them toppled. Blood pooled across the carpet and soaked into it as the victims groaned and pressed their hands to the holes running through them.

For an instant, Elliot and the fake police officer locked eyes again. Both midstride, their focuses keened on one another. When each of them finished their steps, they both knew the chase was over. The fake hurdled the wounded men and burst through exit door. Elliot skidded to a stop and got his hands into the blood.

"Get a first aid kit. Disinfectant, something."

"What are you doing?" Mr. Mink asked. He coughed up blood, but he dug his nails into Elliot's arms and glared. "Go kill that bastard who shot me."

Elliot ignored him and made sure someone else was doing something for the customer that the landlord had sacrificed. Pressure on the wound wasn't the most complicated thing, but he had to talk the helper off the cusp of panic and get them to actually be of use.

Once he could give his attention to Mr. Mink again, he said, "Backup is already on their way. Everything was recorded. EVE will tag him and they'll bag him. Saving your life is more important."

"Fuck that," the landlord said, spitting blood across Elliot's jacket as he spoke. "This ain't enough to do me in. You think I ain't ever been shot before? Go get that bastard."

Someone, the club's star employee for the next month most likely, slammed a first aid kit onto the ground beside Elliot and popped it open. All the usual goods were inside, but it was a big box; it had more than bandages and antiseptics. It had a spray bottle of clotting foam.

Have fun with the surgery.

Elliot cracked the tip open and stuffed it into Mr. Mink's bullet wound. The landlord convulsed and howled before the chemical blasted into his liquefied lung. He squeezed and ripped it out, splattering his shirt with droplets of the rapidly hardening protein. Mr. Mink let go of Elliot and clawed at his own shirt, sweating bullets of pain.

The bleeding was stopped though.

The customer was worse off than the landlord. Having gotten the full brunt of the shot, Elliot could only imagine what had become of the man's intestines. So much blood was on the ground that despite the customer's dark complexion and the dim light, he could still see the pallid color of his face.

"Is he going to be alright?" the impromptu nurse asked. She looked to be on the verge of hyper ventilating.

"Probably," he said, and shoved her shaking hands away. The plastic tube stabbed into the victim's guts. A weak groan came from him as the clotting foam pumped through his insides and out the other hole. The detective bit his lip and felt the man's belly expand.

Probably not, to be honest.

The can sputtered out, and he ripped it free while he still could. The victim's gut looked like a pimple and smelled like a latrine.

The demands of his own body caught up as the adrenaline faded. Half-drunk and half-hungover, bruises burned inside his skin. A moment later, it was his turn to bend over on all fours and puke up half-digested filet mignon.

By the time he cleared out the gagging and coughing, the club had new noises filling it up; the shouts of his fellow police officers storming. Four of them plus a pair of EMTs took control.

"Up here," he croaked, sitting himself down against the wall. He could barely raise his voice, but the recon drone floated beside him, and he hoped someone was actively watching.

Cinder is going to kill me...

17

Profile Analysis of Harold Cuther

2140/06/01

The medical waiting room for vaccination processing was a cold place. The walls had no infographics about common ailments or medicinal advertisements. The side tables had no aged copies of lifestyle magazines, nor educational pamphlets about improving one's health. It was sterile by design to try their patience.

The analog clock had been peculiarly engineered through careful neglect and improper repair such that the only thing accurate about it was the fifteen-minute marks. The second-hand errantly ticked and tocked, rattling in its cage however it happened to feel. The volume varied as it circled the digits and at times it seemed to creep backwards before leaping ahead. Watching it made the passage of time unbearably long for the kids waiting on their compatibility reports.

This of course was part of the interview. Not just him, but the dozen other new adults that sat in hard plastic chairs watching the clock were all recorded and scrutinized for red flag behaviors: the nervous ticks of foot-tapping, a compulsion to sneak nicotine or THC, but, also for anyone who would strike up a conversation among their peers and how successful they were at it. Those were given officer consideration. No one did much of anything during Harry's wait, which made it all the more stifling.

The click of a door latch made them all lift up their heads right at the strike of the hour. "Will numbers four-fifty-six, three-ninety-seven, and three-oh-three please step into the office?" the nurse asked. They each had to check their identification numbers, and at last, it was Harry's turn to rise and leave the hall behind.

Unlike most, Harry had in his hands a print out of opportunities in the armed forces. He had notes and highlights for everything from education to deployment options. He carried the papers like a weapon into the office, and stared at the fogged glass door to the recruitment interview room.

"The three of you are genetically incompatible with the vaccine. You can go home now. Your obligation to your country will be waived," the nurse said as she walked past the three of them and sat back down at her computer.

"What?" Harry, number 303, asked.

Number 456 let out his breath. "You mean I don't have to go to boot camp?"

Number 397 nearly screamed. "Check again. I am not going back to poverty because of a stupid test. There are false negatives you know. Check me again right now," she demanded, grabbing hold of the counter between them and the nurse.

The nurse quietly pressed the button to open the door out and waved them off. When 397 didn't move to leave, she pressed another button and a soldier stepped in to see them out.

Harry took a few steps back, as though the rushing flight of 456 wanted to suck him out the door. He gulped and turned to the soldier. "Is there some way I could just get a posting inside Bastion? Sir, I can't get a job if I'm not a veteran. Not one worth anything anyways."

"Join a corporation. You're young, Three-oh-three. This door is closed though," the soldier said, and shut the door on the three of them.

397 threw a tantrum, and Harry knew well enough to put distance between himself and her. Outside the draft processing center was hardly anything. The one asphalt road in all of Bastion was the ring between the outermost towers and the wall that cut them off from the rest of the world. The processing center sat like a growth off the inner surface and

had a myriad of doors and vehicle entrances that pumped like valves to move people and machines to and fro. The door he and 456 exited was the dirty sphincter of rejection; the one covered in graffiti hatred.

For a moment, he thought he could see a figure watching him through the fogged window above, but the shadow vanished with an overcast cloud, and he had nothing but to walk back into the underbelly of the city.

He tossed his papers in the storm drain.

"What the hell are you doing back, Seventeen?" Miz Pleasant's greeting was as clean as the laundry she was putting back in everyone's rooms. She was in her 'bad clothes', so she still considered herself to be on the clock, but both of them knew what it meant that he was back in the complex already.

"I got rejected," Harry said, and dropped onto the couch. The television had no video streaming hookup anymore, and the only working game console was fifteen years old, but he didn't have the willpower to do anything more than stare at the screensaver.

Miz Pleasant slammed the laundry hamper on the ground and planted her hands on her hips. "What? You got a heart issue you never told me about or something? Did you fail the IQ test? You can't tell me you're too fat for the fitness test."

"I'm not compatible with the vaccine."

Miz Pleasant stared at him. She laughed, a breathless chuckle, as she picked the hamper back up. "Well isn't that some tough shit. I hope you're ready to pack your crap and get out of here."

Harry gritted his teeth and turned to look at her. "You already chased my mother out of here, you leeching hag. Keep pushing me like this and I'll shit down the dryer pipe the next time you clean your fucking lingerie."

Her lips pursed into a sphincter and she jabbed a finger at him. "You've got one week, Seventeen. The minute you're of age, you're on the street. I've got a waiting list, you know that? Dozens of people have applied to live here and they'd actually be grateful. Think about that when you're begging to clean toilets just to put food on your table, you worthless bastard."

A week later, the cleaning machine remained unfouled. Miz Pleasant had let sleeping dogs lie, and he walked out on the street. With only a few hundred credits in his pocket, he found himself standing in front of the government support kiosk. The smiling face of EVE stared back at him. It was painted acrylic, not even a live display screen. He couldn't bring himself to step inside, to grovel for help from the government.

There was a certain calcification of people that ended up in computer mausoleums in Gamma. People with nothing to do, nowhere to go, and nothing in their lives—people like him—that collected like sediment at the bottom of a bottle of beer.

After a month, a man pressed a void mask into his hands. "You need work, don't you?" the similarly masked man asked. "Don't try to say you've got something better to do. I've seen you languish here for a week now. Come on, stand around, run when we run; fifty credits."

Fifty credits was more than what he had in his pocket at that point. The void mask wasn't unfamiliar to him either; here and there people wore the holographic hole to walk through the crowds unseen by EVE's cameras. He said, "Alright," and followed his new benefactor down an alley. The group did a change of clothes out of sight, and then ascended to the thirtieth floor.

That was the first time Harry was accessory to a crime. His unnamed benefactor didn't join them, but a deputized agent led the group up stairs and across bridges until Harry hardly even knew where he was. While he was gawking at an animatronic monster in a sprawling pedestrian mall, the ringleader pulled out an angle grinder the size of a cell phone. The thing was rickety and nearly exploded in his hand, but it managed to slice straight through the chains holding some kind of promo statue.

Harry was stonestruck when he recognized the augmented reality game it was associated with, but then it was in the ringleader's arms, then into his bag.

"Scatter."

The dozen masked up thieves all took different directions and bolted. Only after did anyone notice the device had been stolen and the police summoned. Fear made him run faster and faster, until he vaulted railings and slid down steps and threw himself into the mud of ground floor. The sirens of ARUs filled the air between the towers and hounded him into the darkness.

But then he took the mask off and ditched the clothes. He melted back into the masses and EVE was none the wiser. The all-knowing surveillance state had been beaten, and he had gotten away with it. Only a beating thrill of excitement lingered inside him, and the next night, his benefactor came by the mausoleum to pay him.

With one sentence, he doomed Harold Cuther's future. "There's more where that came from; interested?"

18

Not So Quick Response

2140/09/07

Elliot put the report down and buried his face in his hands. "I arrested a fall guy. A tiny little pawn who doesn't know a single thing beyond his own little anger." He groaned, and took the frustration and bound it back into his chest to puff himself up. "You know, this kid is exactly the kind of person I'm down there to try and help."

Cinder shook her head. "The kid turned down help because of other government branches. Your heroics would never have reached him, Blackstone."

"You don't know that."

Cinder sipped her coffee and stared at him, at the stitches in his hair and the blood across his jacket, the slump of his shoulders. "I should fire you. You know that, right? You gave me like a dozen valid reasons to put your ass on the street."

He sat back in his chair and met her gaze. Gossip leaked through the walls around them. The lights buzzed and the vents rustled with dust and the drop ceiling had water staining, and a thousand other things were annoying about the Missou District Police Station. The pay checks always cashed though, and Cinder had saved his life more times than he could count. "If you fired me, you'd have to explain why I was there in the first place."

The blonde glared back at him. "Nobody asks about someone getting fired for drinking on the job."

Elliot frowned. "I'd sue for wrongful termination. I was working a shift while on painkillers and you knew that."

She sipped her coffee again, slurping the foam. "That wouldn't work for reckless discharge of your firearm."

"I saved two people's lives."

"You let the perp get away."

"The entire active police force let him get away while I was administering first aid."

"That was because of a glitch in EVE's facial recognition software. We still have a bead on him, and he won't get away for long. He's not a ghost, he doesn't have some magic exploit to bypass EVE."

Elliot sighed. "Look, did I keep your lobbyist happy or not?"

Cinder crossed her legs and sipped her coffee once more. She didn't even swallow; she hadn't brought any of it into her mouth, just made the noise while staring at him.

Great, she's thinking it over.

She set the cup down. "Well, he is alive because of you. He was screaming bloody murder... but, his wife calmed him down."

Elliot's eyebrows rose. "That man has a wife?"

Cinder rolled her eyes. "He actually has two wives and a husband. Don't ask me how he got a polygamy license."

"I won't," Elliot said. He sighed and put his elbows on his knees. He stared at the report in front of him.

"So," his boss said, dragging the word out as she watched him. "I hear you were playing that video game instead of having EVE just decrypt it."

Because Devson already crushed the request I put in.

"Hey," Elliot said, slapping his hands together. "Did you find out why I couldn't contact Devson? What is this neural jammer thing anyways?"

Cinder rolled her eyes again. "Not clear. He picked up when I called and said he'd get right on it. You realize that normal people go to sleep at night, don't you? He probably just had a filter set up to get some shut-eye."

I always assumed he was nocturnal though.

"So, what about the neural jammer?" he asked.

She shrugged. "It's been handed over to Daedalus Labs for investigation. Honestly? My money is that they are the ones who cooked it up. It had to have been someone familiar with the operating systems of neural implants because overload filtering is hardcoded."

Elliot scratched the back of his neck and tried to picture pop-up ads appearing directly into his field of view, or how many it would take to cause a seizure like the girl Claire had dealt with. "So, with business habits like that, I imagine the list of suspects against Mr. Mink is pretty long."

Cinder laughed. She bent over to pull open the bottom drawer of her desk and fished out a Zeus energy drink. She cracked it open and sucked it down before the foam overflowed. She had to wipe her lips off before she could say, "Once you include everyone one degree away from any of his business antagonists, the list may as well be half of Bastion. If we can't capture the guy in the mask, the processing required to backtrace everything to the source will be so expensive Mink'd have to appeal directly to Congress."

"Most advanced computer in the world, and it gets defeated by money," Elliot said.

Cinder shrugged. "That's why you get paid, Blackstone; because humans are still cheaper than robots. Also, if anyone actually files a complaint against you, I'm docking your pay to cover the legal fees."

"Oh, come on!"

Cinder ordered him out of her office, and onto Quick Response Standby. Everyone in the station knew what it meant when he slumped over towards the corner elevator up. It was the only way to the top train station. They watched him go, but no one said anything. They politely held their conversations until the gate clicked shut between him and them, then they resumed.

"Oh, hey. I didn't think I'd see-" The elevator door closed and cut off the young woman's voice.

Elliot could hardly keep his eyes open as the lift brought him to the train station. He slumped against the back wall and watched the floor number change. By the time the doors opened, the voice, familiar as it was, had evaporated from his thoughts.

Cigarette smoke filled the glass waiting room beside the train station like a polluted greenhouse. Half a dozen other E-rank officers looked up and laughed when he joined them. They were all in full combat gear, aside from their helmets that were lined up against the wall next to their rifles.

The outfit failed to intimidate when he could see all their faces; the wrinkles, the baby fat, the art tattoos, and most of all the grins.

I'll have to send for my own set before I get called with my pants down.

"Chief finally found a way to keep you out of trouble, Blackstone?" the oldest of the group said. E55146 "Lizard" Wyatt looked like he was ten years past retirement, but was only a few years older than Elliot. Whenever he was asked what he had been through, his answer changed, but Elliot knew it had something to do with a certain visit to California to "meet up with an old friend".

Elliot looked away from his colleagues grin and at the table of cards between the men. "Got room for one more?"

"How much money you got to lose?" the dealer asked. F00135 was a new face to Elliot, but he knew from the badge number that the youth was the newest member of the Missou department. Giving the new guy "Fools" was tradition.

"Are you kidding me? I was getting paid overtime to sit in that club. I've got plenty of money for you to look at while I win," Elliot said, and sat down between the other officers. It took him a moment to figure out which variant of poker they were playing, but soon enough he had a hand, someone had passed him a cigarette, and the midday heat was passing as quickly as money flowed around the table.

"So, what exactly happened to you in the Gaia plant, anyways?" Lizard asked after folding his hand.

Elliot sucked his cig down to the filter and stubbed it out. "Guy by the name of Raffe is... was working a bootleg super-computer out of the basement. I went in to talk with him about this 314 case, and his crazy roommate tried to knife me. Shit hit the fan after that." His hand was looking good, so he bid up.

Fools leaned in, scooping up the discarded cards as he looked at Elliot. "So what's the deal with those goofy masks they were all wearing?"

"The void masks?" Elliot asked, waiting for the betting to come back around too him.

"Yeah, the ones that look like a hole."

"No idea. Hit me, would you?" he asked, and Fools sent him another card. It was useless to his hand, but he didn't let himself flinch. The bruising helped. "It's like a gang thing as far as I can tell, except agnostic of the actual group. If I were you, I'd be worried if I saw one. It's self-dehumanizing."

"That's why Chief Cinder went all guns blazing in there, right? Those thugs didn't stand a chance."

"Once you got in to save me."

Fools squirmed in his seat and shrugged. "Well yeah, the ARU did the heavy lifting, but still, like, that's why we have them, isn't it? To deal with crazy people."

Lizard leaned to the side, peering over his neighbor's cards and squinting his eyes at the pot of money. "What kind of idiots fight back against an ARU?"

Elliot closed his eyes and set his cards face down. "They didn't; they ran. They got shot because they pinged as CZARheads."

Everyone at the table, who hadn't been to his rescue the other night, stared at him. Lizard had been halfway to lighting another cigarette but stopped with it nearly to his lips. "You've gotta be shitting me. A corp was harboring CZARheads? Gaia at that? They're in the fucking food supply."

"Plants can't uptake the virus, and yeast is too simple to infect," Fools said, as though the words regurgitated out of reflex.

Lizard rotated in his seat to stare at the new guy. "Do you have any idea how many people would die if there was an outbreak through the food supply? We're talking hundreds of millions of people, if we got it under control at all. The disease would go exponential and half the people down there? They ain't vaccinated."

All the blood drained from Fools' face. He physically shrank in his seat under Lizard's glare.

"Okay, hold on," Elliot said, lifting up his hand to try and ease Fools' nerves. "It wouldn't be that bad unless the contamination inspection was also compromised. Besides, CZAR is just a derivative of the virus. Even drug dealers know they don't make money if their clients die on them. Everyone knows it's a quick way to get stabbed to death if you sell someone CZAR and they end up infected."

One of the other police officers shoved off the table and rose. "I have to go," she said, covering her mouth and fleeing to get fresh air.

Elliot frowned. "There a story there?"

Lizard lit his cigarette and gave it a puff. "Didn't you hear about the murder case last week?" he asked. "CZAR dealer was found flayed alive and hung from the outer wall. When Cinder found out, she told them to leave it."

"Oh," Elliot said.

I'm surprised that didn't make the news cycle.

Fools leaned over and picked up the abandoned cards. "So, she folded... right?" he asked, and turned her hand over. Full house.

Elliot looked at his own cards again; Three of a kind, Ace high. "Works for me," he said, and revealed his hand. The last other player groaned and flicked his cards at Fools. The new guy scooped the cards, Elliot scooped the pot.

"Deal it up, deal it up," Lizard said. He pulled out his phone and flipped through notifications. Three cops on the street had started streaming from recon drones, but by the time Fools had dealt everyone their cards again, Lizard hadn't found anything that caught his eye. He locked his phone, snatched up his cards, and quickly put his cigarette back in his mouth to hide his smirk.

"Fold," Elliot said, tossing his cards in. He had been dealt a pair right off the bat, but Lizard obviously had something better. Then it was his turn to do the same. Out came his phone, no messages from EVE. He grimaced. His latest escapades hadn't been enough to get her attention, so up came the video streams. The first one he clicked on made him wet his lips and hold up his phone. A bit of jiggling, and it unlocked free camera, so he started panning it about himself to inspect the alley that C00173 "Colt" had found himself in.

It seemed familiar from the moment he saw it. Unfortunately, most of the area was familiar to him, and most of it looked the same outside of corp-controlled blocks. Colt wasn't alone on the ground, his partner was there and the two of them were speaking with a twenty-something local. Blood kept dripping from a ring around his face. Elliot would have been confused how it had happened, if he hadn't first seen the fractured void mask in Colt's hand.

Someone had tried to smash their face in, probably concussed him in the process.

The location clicked into his mind when he saw a schwarma shack and the mustached chef screaming at his customers while dancing knives in his hands.

That's right around the corner from the plantation.

The concussed man was speaking. "Look man, I'm really not here to be filing a police report or anything. I'm not looking for no trouble. Round here, we settle things in house. I know you're just trying to do the right thing and all, and I appreciate you called an ambulance for me, but I'd like to be on my way."

Colt pushed his jacket back and put his hands on his hips. The move exposed the revolver under his arm. "You're awfully chipper for someone who just got their face smashed in. Are you on some kind of drug right now?"

"No, sir." The civilian stared at the ground and shook his head. "I think it's just shock."

"Are you on CZAR?"

The civilian jumped back. "No! No, that's illegal. You get your ass shot for that. Why would I use that stuff?"

Elliot frowned. He had nearly fallen out of his chair to get the right angle. "Speak of the devil," he mumbled.

"What's that?" Lizard asked as he scooped up his meager pot.

"Look's like Colt's on a CZAR bust or something."

The C-rank officer outranked any of them there. What he was doing on the ground was anybody's guess. Colt had his teeth into the civilian though, and he wasn't letting go. "You know, if I were to pull out my plague detector and I got a positive reading, between that and the circumstances... you know what I'd be authorized for, don't you?"

"Sir, I don't use that shit. You see? This, this is why nobody wants you janniseries around here no more. What the hell kind of threat is this just because I got in a scuffle?"

"Fuck," Elliot said, and locked the view. He tossed the phone on the table. "Don't deal me in," he said as Fools started riffling. He left the table and returned to the elevator. One of the few landlines in the city was recessed into the wall beside the lift, and he ripped the phone off its hook. Dial tone rang in his ear. The analog three button rattled when he jammed it. The station quartermaster picked up on the other end. "It's Elliot. Can you send up a set of QRS gear for me?"

"Rifle, shotgun, or crowd control?" the old stock keeper asked.

Elliot twisted around and peered at the row of weapons. His side twinged within the rib brace. "Make it crowd control."

"So that would be the happy face, not the skull, right?"

For the love of-

"Is neither an option?"

The quartermaster laughed. "Sure, sure. I got just the thing for you. Do you need me to send more sidearm ammo for you too? Since you seem to be shooting everyone you meet nowadays."

Elliot thunked his forehead against the rim of the phone box. "No, I'm alright on that front."

"Alright, just checking. I'm calling the lift now. It'll be up when it gets up there."

Elliot slammed the phone back into its rest and marched back to the table. The game had dragged to a halt. Everyone was watching the stream.

"Kid's clean," Lizard said.

Fools said, "Colt pulled the detector out; got nothing."

"The guy's from the Gaia plantation, isn't he?"

Lizard nodded. "Betting money says so."

Fools held up his phone. A grainy, infrared slugfest played out. "Found this from querying EVE. Visual cameras are all broken in the area, but this one here, the one getting his ass beat, is the guy Colt's talking to."

"So who's the other one?"

"Getting there, getting there," the new guy said, and turned his phone back around to pull up another window. "Check it out, caught him on a wifi pass about fifty meters away. Sergei Djin; he's on Cinder's short list."

"Short list?"

"Of people with a motive to have shot Mr. Mink." Fools grinned so much Elliot could have counted his cavities.

Well that explains why Colt was walking. Just how big does Cinder think this mask group is?

"Lovely; just the kind of person I want to get called in for."

Lizard dragged on his cigarette till the ash crumbled off. He stubbed the filter into the ash tray and shook his head. "We never get called for anything else. Come on, let's get in the train."

The lift dinged and opened up while everyone else was strapping their helmets on. Elliot walked back over to get his things. He stopped cold a step away from the pile.

The quartermaster had supplied him a helmet, and it was neither the happy face nor a skull. It was set to a bunny face, leftover from Easter.

You've gotta be kidding me.

"Blackstone! Get a move on. Train's ready to go."

He picked it up, animal mask and all, and joined them on the train to descend into the bowels of the city.

19

The Modern Printing Press

2140/09/07

"Look mom, circus man!"

The child, six years old at the most, was hushed up by her mother and moved along. Exactly as the mask had been designed, it distracted the kids from the bullet proof armor, the pistol at his hip, and the array of road closure signs warning anyone from trying to sneak past him and end up where the shoot-out raged.

Well, at least if my identity does get leaked from this, people won't be so hostile to me anymore. They'd just be laughing at me for being the bunny-man. That'd be much better...

He stood between a pair of flashing pylons. "Due to ongoing police activity, this area is temporarily closed. We are sorry for the inconvenience, but it is for your own safety." The pylons looped that announcement every thirty seconds. He could have sped it up, but it would have driven him insane. Any slower, and people might not hear it before stumbling into him. One would-be journalist came jogging over to it like a fly to shit.

The man was short and kept his head shaved. The tattoos around his neural implant scar replaced his hair. By the looks of his clothes, Elliot pegged him as a cityboarder; all mismatched patches of neon. "What's going on here, officer?" he asked, shoving a camera at Elliot and trying to peer over his shoulder. Nothing was visible; the showdown was around a corner to keep an entire tower between him and wandering bullets.

Elliot held up a steel-clad glove to keep the journalist at bay. "This area is closed. Only first responders are allowed in. This is for your own safety."

"Come on man," the journalist said. He jumped from side to side, as though that would get him around the blockade. "I'm a reporter for the Tenn Independent. Freedom of the press, right? I gotta get in there and see what's brought the MPs down."

Elliot put his hand into the man's chest and pushed him back. The extra weight the armor gave him made it tiresome to walk, but when he needed to be a wall it was very handy. "Look, I don't care if you're the Commander's son. I'm not to let anyone through until the area is secured."

To punctuate his sentence, a gunshot went off. The report echoed around the corner, and then the QRS team responded with a hail of returning fire. The crack of rifles and the pop of shotguns filled the air like static noise, and the journalist jumped back.

Well someone just died.

"It's for public safety," Elliot said.

The journalist eyed him up and down. Some gears shifted in his head, and he focused the camera on Elliot instead. "So what's the deal with the animal mask?"

"It's not an animal mask."

"Sure looks like one."

"This is a standard QRS helmet set to a kid friendly holographic appearance. I'm the one politely telling people to stay away, right? Would you expect kids to listen if I walked around looking like a killer robot?"

"Don't you normally use happy smiles for that instead?"

Son of a bitch, a journalist who actually knows what he's talking about.

Elliot glanced over his shoulder. It was too far away to be heard, but he could see an ARU climbing down the wall of a tower, descending to the firefight with guns drawn. It picked its way over bridges and between support struts for the train lines. The journalist saw it too, and snapped a picture.

The detective shook his head. "What did you say your name was?"

The journalist stuck his hand out to shake. "Peter Esteban. Tenn Independent's top on the ground reporter for the Missou district."

Never heard of him

"Peter," Elliot said without shaking his hand. "Do you do a lot of ambulance chasing?"

Peter retracted his hand. "Police activity chasing, yeah. It's rare and bloody when you people come down here and if we left it up to the automatic reporting, nobody would know. You people would just get the sys-admins to scrub all the embarrassing things."

As if anyone would bother with that. No one reads that crap.

"You know we come down here in uniform. Even plain clothes sometimes. And we face a whole lot of hostility when we do. Did you ever think that your focus on..." he glanced back in the direction of the firefight. No one had shot since the main volley, but the noise had left a void in its wake. The din of life was on hold. "Volatile action is having unintended consequences?"

Peter pursed his lips into a frown. "Did you ever think that it's a product of you competing with private security forces? You know, up above in the Alpha strata, I know you police officers still handle the routine stuff, the shaking of hands and the smiles, and I'm sure you've got a great reputation with those rich folks. When the only thing down here you do is get into shootouts with... let me guess; contraband smugglers?"

"They haven't made an official statement yet. Someone is being apprehended on suspicion of another event," Elliot said.

"Right, so anyways, you come down to get into these shootouts and what? You expect people to have a good impression of you?" Peter asked.

"The only reason people think what we come down here for is to shoot them, because people like you put a spotlight on it. You know, you could be helping with investigations, right? Half the cameras down here have been smashed to pieces; we still have to talk to people down here if we're to find anyone. Why don't you put a spotlight on that?"

The journalist huffed and turned his camera away. "Why the hell do you think, jannis? Nobody is going to pay money for that kind of boring shit."

Elliot leaned in and jabbed the journalist with his finger. "So you care more about the money than about the news. Get the fuck out of here before you get shot by a drug dealer."

Peter stepped back, and turned his head this way and that way. He looked like a corvid scoping out for a rat as he checked all the other bridges and staircases. The journalist didn't say anything as he backpedaled and vanished around a corner.

Seriously?

Elliot tapped a few buttons on the side of his helmet to cycle the internal view. He could see straight out of the visor, but there were transparent overlays. On command, it synchronized with EVE and put a bead right on the journalist as the man went running through halls and alleys to circle round. The effect was similar to what neural implants did, or so he had been told.

The detective backtracked into the secured zone, stepped onto the other walkway, and crossed his arms. A moment later, an out of breath journalist skidded to a stop in front of him. "What are you looking at, Bunny Mask?"

"You're not allowed in the area. If you break in, you will be arrested," Elliot said.

His radio crackled in his ear. "Blackstone," Lizard said. "We've still got no dice on the ringleader. Watch the ARU, we're going to be on the move."

Elliot turned back. From the new spot, he could see down to the broken, mud-covered train stop that had become their focal point. Ever since the suspended rails had been built, the ground trams had become obsolete, and he was reasonably sure if they tried to send a car there directly, the thing would crash. After a decade of disuse, it almost looked like outside the city; it even had weeds growing in the cracks. Four officers—Colt included—milled around half a dozen locals. Each of them was on their knees, hands pressed against a security shutter for an out-of-business phone store.

"What do you mean you still haven't gotten him? Did he drop off the scanners?"

Lizard grumbled. "The sonofabitch killed his neural implant. We're not even getting residuals."

The mental image of a removable skin flap to access the fuel cell made Elliot's stomach lurch. "Then how are you planning to catch him?"

"I don't know, ask EVE."

The AI chimed in directly to their conversation. "The suspect took the battery out of their phone as well, but they seem to have forgotten that their wireless earbuds are still powered on in their pocket."

Note to self...

"Alright EVE, put him in my mask, would you?" Elliot asked. "I'll try to pen him in."

"Officer," the AI responded, "he's headed directly your way."

The colored triangle marking the vector to the target's position appeared at the side of Elliot's vision and he spun his head. It went to a small fire escape—repurposed to general use—and a man in a black hoody walking down it slightly faster than normal.

"Bastard's blood, send the ARU over, will you? And EVE, consider putting a blackout on this journalist. Name of Peter Esteban," he said, and started walking towards the target.

The journalist couldn't hear him—the speaker system disabled whenever the radio was in use—but he could see the change in Elliot's attitude. Quite the professional, out came the camera. He shadowed Elliot, peering ahead to get a shot at anyone and anything he seemed to be approaching.

Elliot glanced over his shoulder at the trailing journalist who had just broken the police perimeter. "Congratulations, you just committed a crime. Are you going to run?"

"We got a bail fund at the Independent."

If only I had the time to deal with him. Where's Fools when you need him... actually...

"Hey Fools," he said into the common channel. "Get over here and arrest this trespasser, will you?"

The new guy didn't respond at first, but when his voice came through it was in the slurred rush of someone who had fumbled the mute button. "Yes, sir. Coming to your position now."

"Just follow the ARU," he said, and thumbed off the radio. The target was right ahead of him. He held up his hand. "Excuse me, sir. Military Police. I have a few questions for you."

In his experience, it was about one in twenty times that the perpetrator actually stopped to speak when confronted. One in two innocent people would stop, while the other half fled for something unrelated. The man in front of him didn't break stride until he put his foot on the ground floor.

With both feet on the ground, the man twisted and bolted.

Elliot gave chase without surprise. The twenty kilos of equipment and bruises slowed him down though. Despite what some controlled tabloids speculated, QRS gear didn't actually have any mechanized support, and the most he could do was get a wheezing, lumbering chase down the road.

It was the ARU that did the real work. The machine barreled past him at full speed. On flat ground, it forwent the inhuman, spider-like maneuvering and instead charged foot over foot like a charging lion. Elliot heard the cycling of guns beneath its chassis as it ran past, and then it stopped by somersaulting and grinding to a halt. It spun to face the perp, and started its script. "Stop, you are under arrest and hereby detained-"

If it had shot instead of spoke, it might have stopped the perp in time. In the midst of that delay, the man produced a conical hammer from his pocket and smashed through a display window. Glass went everywhere, and he fled inside the complex.

"Go! Get in there," Elliot shouted, waving at the ARU.

The machine wavered like a restrained hound, nudging towards the gaping hole but couldn't go.

The building wasn't public. It had the bright yellow banding Elliot was all too familiar with; Phoenix Construction. Given the exclusive contract to build not only the towers of Bastion, but the infrastructure layer beneath it all, they employed every trade worker in North America, or so they claimed. People here and there knew how to fix leaking pipes or put down a weld, but it was the legions of workers for Phoenix that kept the city functioning.

The perp had broken into one of their residential blocks. He had smashed open the window to their cafe and gone running into the hydroponic garden. An alarm was already going off internally. Elliot could hear the ding-dong chime bringing the Phoenix Security force to attention.

It just had to be Phoenix, didn't it? At least I'm in the bunny mask. Nobody will want to shoot a nice, friendly bunny man, right?

20

Social Justice

2140/09/07

The Phoenix apartment complex was as stylish as it was hospitable to outsiders. They did, however, have one of the most unique layouts in all of Bastion. With the freedom that came from knowing the exact loading paths of the structure, the interior architects had clumped rooms together throughout the tower, leaving fluctuating space between them. The effect would have been like a cave system, if not for all the garden plants spilling over the balconies and laden with tomatoes, squash, and so on.

The residents watched the one idiot who had thought the tower would make a clever escape route. The corporation's avatar watched too. Less of a trend chaser than companies like Gaia, Phoenix had only recently bent to the latest zeitgeist. Tori, as their avatar was called, looked down across the courtyard with quiet disdain, half her face hidden behind fire-red hair. The display screen she used was nearly large enough to have a home at Liberty Stadium. She was a giant overlooking the complex.

"We seem to have an uninvited guest today," she said, her voice echoing throughout the tower.

I can't even tell whether that's a computer or not.

Tori held up a hand like a mob boss signaling her killers. "Would the local security forces please step forward?"

Elliot hadn't been in a particular rush. Even though the man he was chasing had been sprinting, there was no longer anywhere for him to go. Every hall, every bridge, every path suddenly had a worker twice his size standing between him and escape. He even went so far as to jump off the second story balcony, land in the middle of a flower bed, and bolt for an ice cream parlor that had a through door. The old man working the scoops pulled a shotgun on him the moment he tried, and the two kids eating laughed.

"Well, it seems we have two guests actually," Tori said, and her digital gaze fell on Elliot. He was only one step out of the coffee shop, but he still felt half a dozen gazes fall onto him. The avatar smiled. "An old friend of the company, you might say. He's being polite at the moment, so don't be rough with him. This... other one though. We need to do something about him."

Elliot's heart hammered and he reflexively put a hand to his chest, where his badge would have been.

Right, machine. Must have scanned something.

The man backtracked, finding himself in the middle of the courtyard with security forces all around him. He was breathing hard and held up his hands. "Come on, come on, you know me. You people know me."

Who the hell would admit to knowing a criminal in their own home? He's going to get himself killed.

A hand grabbed hold of Elliot's shoulder and he turned halfway around. A too-familiar face stared at him. Mr. Hoppes, the security officer he had run into at the computer mausoleum, gave him a nod. "We've got this, officer," he said.

Can't imagine he'd be this polite if he could see past the mask.

He activated a voice filter, and said, "He's a wanted suspect. We need him for questioning. If you can authorize the ARU to enter, we can detain him for you."

The man nodded and scratched his chin. He seemed to be thinking it over. Then Elliot heard a clang of steel and the man screaming in pain.

He spun. A heavy, galvanized pipe clattered away across the floor as the perp fell to the ground clutching his leg.

It bent halfway between his knee and his ankle.

Elliot groaned.

"What the hell?" a man the size of a gorilla asked as he walked over to the squealing man. "You lactose intolerant or something? Or have you just never lifted something heavy?"

"You son of a bitch." The perp rolled, scattering mud from one of the vegetable pots as he tried to squirm away. "Rhyme, what are you doing to me? I just needed to pass through. I sold you amphetamines literally yesterday."

Smuggler, great.

The large man rolled his eyes and shook his head. "Come on man, you can't just go and shout something like that and expect to get help. Don't you know better? Did you start snorting some of that Asian crack or something?"

Tori's gaze fell on him. "Rhyme, you wouldn't be using performance inhibiting drugs while on duty, would you be?" the artificial girl asked.

He spun around to face her and put his hands behind his back. "No ma'am. Stimulants only. I'm clean. No CZAR either."

The perp tried to scramble away, his face contorted with pain whenever his broken leg moved. Another security officer walked over and put a boot onto his back, pinning him to the ground. They didn't have a gun, but they weren't unarmed either. A stun baton like a cattle prod crackled in their grasp and made the perp's hair stand on end.

Elliot looked over at the man standing beside him, the one he had gotten into a fight with. "You're not looking to detain him, are you?"

The security officer used his chin to point at Tori. "That's up to her, not me."

"No," she answered. "I don't think it would benefit us in the slightest to keep a lowlife like this inside our home. Your companions are assembling outside, Officer. Why don't you hand over your cuffs and we can toss him on the street for you?"

Elliot held up the steel cuffs and the man took them from him. The perp gave up on escaping and resolved to keep his mouth shut. Elliot would have watched the wrangling and the chicken-winging, but Tori's gaze had been locked on him ever since. "Normally I would ask why the police department had fallen so low as to let someone run this far but I understand you actually have an excuse."

A small screen beside Elliot flashed and mirrored Tori's figure. It had been a menu display for the coffee shop, so still and dim he had mistaken it for a sign. Then the avatar of the corporation stood next to him. Rather than a mere face shot, he could see her entire body and the impossible, feathery dress she wore. At life-size, the intensity of her gaze was only a half step removed from real.

"What can I say?" the detective said. "Trouble has a way of finding me lately. It's really getting in the way of my day job."

"Well, we will be happy to have you out of here and back to... whatever it is you consider your day job. Would that be trudging through the rain by yourself in the middle of the night?"

He grimaced. "You could say that."

She smirked.

Who the hell is behind this one? This the boss that Cinder messaged to get me off the hook?

She said, "Just so you know, we have plenty of cameras of our own around here. Unlike our competition; Phoenix Construction keeps our own in line. You won't get stabbed by a tweaked out CZARhead."

Elliot nodded and surveyed the area again. Bystanders had appeared in windows and doorways, peaking around corners and watching the show. They were kids mostly; Dom's age. "I can see how having those around would cause issues for your employees."

"We at Phoenix Construction like to build more than just the towers we live in. We do what we can to help our employees build their lives, their relationships. We think of it as paying them with more than money."

To pay them less money, I would assume.

"What's that got to do with me?"

Tori smiled. "We reviewed the altercation the other night and determined that the video evidence was of too low quality to pursue. It would appear that a favorable glitch in the system has occurred for you. Your problem has disappeared. You can go back to being the hero for kids."

Elliot rocked back on his heels. "I'm sure the kids will appreciate that."

"Precisely, Officer."

"I don't suppose, as you were reviewing all your footage, that you could tell me anything about these void masks I keep seeing? There are kids wearing them, and video game developers are using them. Got any of those around here? They seem to pop up even more than CZAR."

The smirk turned into a pout. "Some kids bring them in from time to time. Nothing more."

He glanced over at the perp and saw the security officers hauling him up to what passed for standing. Elliot nodded. "Alright then. I'll get out of here." He turned away from the avatar and turned on his radio. A moment after his request, and Colt walked in to carry the perp out with him.

The man grunted and sagged in their grasp the moment they both had arms through his chicken wings. He dragged his good leg across the ground, and couched his broken one up as they hauled him back to the ARU.

"Officer," Tori said as they passed. "There's an old saying we at Phoenix still remember; never get between a man and his money. If you deprive him of how he makes a living, you've killed him. Hopefully, the next time we see you, things won't be so violent, yes?"

"Hopefully," Elliot said, and glanced at Mr. Hoppes, standing around and watching the real police officers work. The man frowned back at him, none the wiser.

When they stepped out onto the street, Colt looked at him. "Good work, Blackstone," Colt said, but Elliot's attention was utterly gone.

This situation with the masks and the gangs... it's just going to get bigger and bigger. The whole department is getting sucked in ever since they tried to kill Mr. Mink. Nguyen's going to just get forgotten if I don't do something about it.

Elliot looked around at the QRS squad gathered next to the ARU. Some were busy speaking into their radios, coordinating in a train car to take them back to the station and others were on crowd control. They had the situation under control.

A convenient glitch in the system to make your problem go away? That's a little too convenient, isn't it? And the glitch is where no glitch should ever be...

"You know, I never thought I would say this, but I have to go play a video game before it's too late."

"What? You're knocking off? Not gunna see this one through?" Colt asked.

"Yeah, I've got a prior investigation I need to wrap up. Fools! Get over here, I need you to take this guy," Elliot shouted, and waved the new guy over.

The other officers watched silently, and he was sure Colt was calling in a complaint about it to Cinder, but Elliot turned his back to them and popped his helmet off. He pulled out his phone, dialed, pressed it to his ear and said, "Hey, Mikey. You home? I need to borrow your son's computer again."

21

End Credits

2140/09/07

Elliot resolved himself to never admit how long he spent trying to beat [The Faceless Well]. It took him over an hour to work out how to get the sword again, and then two tries to actually slay the beast. It seemed smarter than the first time, but not so much that he couldn't hack it apart like a hungover butcher. He didn't get interrupted when he finally swung a leg over the edge of the well and planted it on the rusted iron rung. Hand over hand, he descended into the darkness beneath the puppet hamlet.

The wall faded from sight and then from existence. He nearly fell when he realized he had nothing but a series of handles floating in the air. The rest of his steps were made with a white-knuckled grip on every rung until he finally felt water beneath him. Not a pool from which to draw water from, but more like a water slick over concrete.

The stone and dirt walls of the well couldn't even be seen over his head. Aside from the shaft of light descending upon him, he couldn't see anything at all about him.

Is it incomplete? Did I do all of that for nothing?

The simulation shuddered. The lag in processing made his senses lurch as though in an earthquake. Then the ground moved. The darkness bloomed with diffuse light across a slew of grass topped rubble. A path formed in front of him, rising up from the base of the simulation. The chunks of material made a staircase suspended in the air, but proved solid under his feet.

"Familiar, isn't it?"

Elliot glanced around, but the voice didn't have a source. The audio data had been fed directly to him like a narrator.

"This cobblestone path. You've probably walked over it a thousand times and never truly thought twice about it. It's just part of the game. But, the thing is, it's part of almost every game. This isn't even what cobblestone looks like. This is," the narrator said. The cadence of his words seemed to be timed with Elliot's steps, so he took an easy pace and listened. He listened and watched as new materials formed beneath his feet.

The change in cobblestone was distinct. Rather than a mix of rocks stuck into the ground and held fast by weedy dirt, he stepped onto masonry cut squares. The path was smooth, with barely a curve to it to shed water.

"Or, I could go back even further in time, to this," the narrator said.

The path changed again, switching to enormous boulders that had been worn smooth by foot traffic. Some even had ruts cut into them from centuries of carts. It felt like he was marching over a mountain.

"But you don't ever see those, do you? And that's not any one person's fault, least of all your perceptiveness. The truth is, cobblestone is annoying to make and it doesn't add much to the experience by itself. So game developers, like myself, prefer to download someone else's craft and use that. It lets us do more rewarding things, like figure out how to delude the player into losing track of time."

Nguyen... where are you.

The path switched to cracked asphalt as he continued to rise through the darkness. Around him, bits and pieces of simulated worlds floated by like driftwood in a river. Some he recognized from B:GONE, others from games he played as a child. Most may as well have been meaningless.

"But you see, that's the problem. The cobblestone is just one example. If you keep your eyes open though, you'll find the same missable models in all kinds of games, regurgitated like scene dressing to keep you from thinking about your experience too much. Sure; the set pieces will get their own tender love and care. But, isn't that like putting a new face on the same body? Here, don't you recognize this body?" Nguyen said as Elliot finally came to a platform of sorts.

One of the mannequins from above stood at attention before him, under its own spotlight. When he took a step closer, it sprouted flesh. The posture didn't change, but an instant later an average man of average height and complexion stood looking back at him in nothing more than underwear. The only thing about it that would have made Elliot notice the man on the street was that he was standing upright, rather than slouching.

"Behold," Nguyen said. "Human Male One, the test file NPC used in every crowd generator available on the market. Theoretically, he's used as a sanity check; if your game can't work with Human Male One, it's the game that is broken not the model. Therefore, everyone uses him, because why waste the effort making someone new? That would cut into corporate profits, don't you know?"

A guillotine axe fell from the sky and cleaved off the face of Human Male One. The metal slammed into the ground with a clamor, and Elliot jumped back. No blood sprayed out at him; the face simply disappeared and left a hole behind where it should have been.

Human Male One looked like he was wearing a void mask.

Elliot heard footsteps to his side, and turned to see a fully animate figure strolling past him, walking up to Human Male One. Richard Nguyen did not strike an impressive figure. He was tall and thin for lack of exercise. He kept a scraggly beard that didn't even cover his jaw and his black hair sat in a busy ponytail down his back.

"You see, the thing is that people get into this industry out of passion. There's art. A means of expression that engages with people more viscerally than anything else possible. Passion doesn't put food on your table though. Passion doesn't buy you someone else's talents to use and augment your own skills. Passion doesn't buy you the latest rendering engines or the latest emotion programs. You have to make money," Nguyen said as he paced around the detective and the NPC.

Elliot scratched his chin and didn't take his eyes off the recorded figure of the murder victim. There might have been planned interactivity, but for as long as it would talk, he would listen.

"You have to monetize somehow. Everyone knows that. There's no way around it. Even if it's just begging for donations from people who enjoy your work. I thought that microtransactions would be fine; non-mechanical alterations in style. Innocent things. Some of it was even marketing, like including NPC skins based on various entertainers. And in the end, it worked. My game turned a profit. It turned an enormous profit actually. It was so much that the competition literally could not afford to ignore us, and they tried to buy Village of Beasts off of me."

Elliot's jaw dropped.

Nguyen had a bit of a smirk to his face. "Of course," he said, wagging his finger in the air. "By that point, I had released the first expansion, turning it into Beastville with some optimizations to the gameplay loop, and I had already announced the Grand Order expansion. You might be asking yourself something though; why don't I look like the guy credited with the game's creation? B:GONE, as it's known now, is hugely successful. People literally make a living through playing it. When you look up the background on it, the man credited with its creation is one Steve Devson, and he sold it to Dimeworks for at least seven figures. I am not Steve Devson... as shocking as that may be to some of you."

Cue the laugh track? Sorry I don't feel like laughing for a dead man.

"I'd like to ask you a question," Nguyen said, walking closer to Elliot. The phantom of a dead man stared him in the eyes. "Did you have fun getting here?"

"Hell no," Elliot said. Irritation bubbled up inside him, and he huffed, put his hands on his hips, and stared back at the program.

Nguyen smiled. "So it was a bit hard for you, was it? Did you find it unfair? To not have your hand held and get eased into the world? Were you expecting explanations and guidance? A set of challenges gradually increasing in difficulty? Was it a shock that you could challenge the monster at any time? That it was entirely up to you to decide what to do with yourself to deal with it? Because, if you will, that monster is like releasing your baby into the harsh waters of the free market. You can do it at any time, and no one is there to really tell you whether you're doing anything right. And I don't know if you noticed this, but there is no limit to what you can do before you challenge the monster. Given your playtime, I suspect you did very little at all before coming here. Are you in a rush?"

Elliot leaned closer and sneered. "You expect me to stop and smell fake roses or something? Come on, I came here to get justice for your death, not to hear about this crap."

"I'd like to let you know that you can replay this game as much as you'd like. Nobody is going to tell you that you have to beat the game. That's really not the point, you know? This isn't a narrative game. There's no story. This is an experience and you rushed to the end. Did it feel like you got your money's worth? Is that the feeling you wanted to have? Some people are like that; they measure their life by money. How much they have, how much they make, what they're worth... and some people would do just about anything in pursuit of it. Even stab their friend in the back."

Replaying this is the last thing I will ever do.

Nguyen smiled and put his hand to his chin. "My name is Richard Nguyen, and there is a reason you don't know who I am," he said, and he pulled his own face off like a mask. Only a hole looked back at Elliot. "Steve Devson deleted me for profit."

22

First Day Of Death

2138/03/15

"Sir, your credit card has been declined…"

Nearly two dozen people were queued up behind Richard. They shifted around, flipping through websites on their phones or gazing into the abyss of their neural implants. The line had a cadence of approach; a glacial approach towards the smell of coffee and pastries. His monetary stumble wasn't even noticed. They pressed closer.

"What do you mean declined? I barely use this card," he asked, taking it back from the barista. He squinted and read the expiration date; he still had two years on it. "Did you run it again?"

The girl shrugged and glanced over his shoulder. There was a very large man behind him playing a game on his phone, expecting to pick up his order. "I tried three times. Do you have a chip?"

Richard leaned over the counter to look at the computer. It was the computer that did all the real work; the girl was just for the human element. The error message didn't say 'card declined' it said 'account not found'. He scratched his whiskery beard. "Only crazy people have credit chips in this day and age."

"Well, if you don't have another means of payment-"

"I have a smart wallet on my phone. Can't I use that?" he asked, and produced the old device. Before she could answer, he tried logging in.

"Account not found."

The girl winced. "I'm sorry sir, but I'll have to ask you to step aside so I can serve the other customers."

The presence of the man behind him could be felt by bodyheat alone. Richard slipped away with his head down and his stomach empty. The smartwallet program had a customer support line, and he dialed them up as he walked out of the cafe. As he stepped out into the sweeping boardwalk across the fiftieth floor—signing business contracts basically required an office so high up—he went through all the motions of the computer receptionist.

The machine didn't find his account, but put him in queue for a human representative. The wait was immense, and he switched to a headset as he walked to the train station. His office was a good few kilometers away still, so he queued up with the rest of the bureaucrats of Bastion. Scanning his phone at the turnstile, to check his full access pass, turned up a glaring red X. His waist thumped into the bar holding him back and it didn't budge.

The woman behind him groaned, her own phone mere centimeters away from the scanner as she boxed him in to the turnstile. "Sorry," he said, and scanned again. It failed. He pulled his phone out of its protective case and directly pressed it to the scanner. It failed.

Station Security walked over to him with a frown. "If you don't have a pass, you can buy one over there," he said, pointing to the teller machines.

Cheeks burning, Richard squeezed backwards through the line and walked over to the ticket machine. They were so disused they actually had dust on them. Everyone halfway up the city lived with permanent passes like he was supposed to have. Most just used computer recognition with their neural implants. He had to buy a single use pass to get across town, except he didn't have a working credit card.

He started walking.

Eventually, the phone operator picked up the call and once again, Richard had to repeat all the inane questions about who he was and what his issue was. "Could you please read off your account number for me?" the lady asked.

He did so, with a few glances to see if anyone was recording him.

"Sir, we don't have any record of ever having had an account with that number. Which... I suppose is strange because it's a valid number. The checksum algorithm checks out, but it's not tied to anything. How did you get this number?"

He licked his teeth, flared his nostrils, and said, "Because it's my account. Isn't that what I told you? This is my credit line. I've used it every day for five years now. Why is it suddenly gone? Did you have a data breach or something?"

"No sir, we maintain all of our records with the highest quantum encryption possible. Would you like me to transfer you to our fraud department? There's nothing I can do for you. If you would like to open up a new account however, I can process that."

"Transfer me, please."

By the time he was walking past the memorial to the last president—the 44th—the fraud department picked up and once again asked him all the identifying questions. "So you think you've been the victim of some kind of identity theft?" the man on the other end of the line asked.

Richard rolled his eyes. "I wouldn't call it theft; more like destruction."

"I can see that, given your name didn't turn up any records at all. Normally, I'd hang up on you as a presumed scammer, but honestly this is the first time I've run into this kind of scam, so I'm curious."

Richard stamped his foot. "It's not a scam. I mean... It's somebody's scam but it's not mine. I'm the victim here. Can't you pull me up by my bank account?"

The fraud department worker sighed. "Sir, please keep your temper under control. It's not going to help the process at all. Do you want to give me your citizen ID again and I can run it through EVE?"

Richard stopped in the presidential statue's shadow. The Great Orator, although none of his speeches had survived the outbreak, stared out across the suspended plaza, a steel gaze to the horizon that went right over his head. The plaque discussing his death in office became Richard's seat as he once again tried to identify himself.

The city AI joined the conversation to say, "I am sorry, but no record exists for that citizen ID."

Richard licked his lips and closed his eyes as he thought it over. "EVE, are you still on the line?"

"This is EVE's ghost from Relay Nine."

The local instance of the AI's processing was good enough. "You can drop the credit company off the call. Are you able to see me right now?"

After a moment, the AI responded, "I am able to see the person holding the phone I am speaking with, yes."

Richard glanced around. He spotted the camera looking at him, a glossy eye built into a fake owl. Bastion had no real owls, but the vermin didn't know that. "Do you not know who I am if you can see me?"

"No data is known about the person I am looking at. It is possible you are either from the Isles, or a foreign nation."

He cracked his knuckles one by one and stared back at the camera. "If that were true, you would have record of my ingress to Bastion."

"Unless you're a smuggler or human trafficker. It is a well-known fact that the walls of Bastion are porous. I advise everyone to write their politicians regarding-"

"I'm not," he interjected. "I haven't been hiding myself up here either. Play back your tapes and backtrace me, why don't you? You knew who I was yesterday, so when did you forget?"

For five minutes, he sat listening to hold music; the equivalent of the AI humming. For five minutes, hundreds of people walked past him without even glancing over at him. For five minutes, he sat waiting to find out if he even existed.

"Well," EVE said, "it seems like you came from an apartment that isn't registered to anyone, which is illegal, and I have no record of any violation reports that would have been generated by this discrepancy. If no one lived there, registration should have defaulted to the landlord. I don't have any held records from yesterday, as too much time has since passed. Without a valid reason, I can't store data that long. If I had detected you walking around, you would have been flagged as a smuggler, like you are now, which implies that at the time I knew who you were. This is highly strange. I believe you may have been the unfortunate victim of data corruption. A cosmic ray perhaps?"

He sank down till his head was between his knees. He couldn't speak. He closed his eyes and shut out the world, but it was all still there when he opened them again. "Can you do something about that?"

"I will have to file a request with my system administrators. This could take up to a week to resolve, possibly longer. My apologies. Your status has been switched to Unknown rather than a potential smuggler, but I have to warn you that if you partake in any illegal activity during this time, systems such as the police ARU will not view you as having human rights. You're essentially not a human right now. More like one of the blighted outside."

Richard hung up on the AI and closed his eyes again. When he opened them anew, a new advertisement had scrolled across the billboard overlooking the plaza. It was high overhead, and painted the area in a new hue, fighting even the rising sun. Call of Honor : Blood and Sand, created by Dimeworks, sponsored by the New California Armed Forces, loomed everyone with camouflaged giants. Despite being an alternate history game of Afghanistan Skunk Works, the models looked like random people off the street.

He could see the camera stationed beneath the billboard, scanning the plaza and mirroring people's faces up above to catch their attention and sell the latest rendition of make-believe war. There was even a disclaimer about loot boxes scrolling across the bottom, absolving them of legal responsibility for marketing gambling to minors.

He licked his dry lips. The hair on the back of his neck stood up and his chest tightened.

Richard Nguyen took off running all the way to his office. He slipped in the first door behind someone else and ran past the front companies. His studio was in the back, and when he reached the door—locked of course—he pounded his fist on it. "Devson! Devson, I know you're in there."

No response came. He looked at the door once more; the glass sheet with his name painted onto it. Then he punched through it. Shards of glass ripped through his skin and more exploded across the ground. A security alarm went off as he reached in and opened the door from within. Glass crunched beneath his shoes as he marched in to find his business partner.

"What the fuck are you doing?" Steve Devson asked as he came walking out of the beta testing room.

"What did you do?" Richard demanded, jabbing his partner in the chest with a bloody finger. His hand stung like hell, burning more with every moment. It made his snarl all the more genuine.

Devson hesitated. He glanced over his shoulder at the hallway in. "What did I do? I made a deal with the biggest playmaker in the industry, in the whole world even."

"I told you we weren't selling to Dimeworks. You saw the play numbers same as me. Why the fuck don't you understand that the Beastville they want to make is one step away from raw poison?"

Devson laughed. "Richie, Richie, just because people like playing your game doesn't mean it's a bad thing. It's the exact opposite. If you had just seen it that way from the start, we wouldn't be having the slightest disagreement." The man grinned, his thin lips almost looking purple.

Richard wanted to tear his own heart out. "We are an entertainment company; not a drug dealer. We sell fun, not addiction! I should have fucking fired you, bought you out, whatever it took." he screamed. "God damn it, you were my friend. I trusted you. You and me against the market. Wasn't that what we agreed? What happened to that?"

JAMES KRAKE

| 160 |

Devson shrugged. "It's a bit late for that though, isn't it? Judging by how angry you are, I'm sure you've already noticed. This isn't your company anymore. It's mine, and I sold B:GO for top dollar, and you know what that did for me? It bought me a seat as a system administrator for EVE. You can do all kinds of things when you have direct access to the entire city."

The police didn't need to follow their WPS maps, they could follow their ears. Richard Nguyen was screaming and trying to smash his way through the bathroom door of his office with a plastic stool to get at Devson inside. The first thing they did when they saw him, was pull up his profile, and got told only that he was an Unknown.

So they shot him in the back with a tazer round.

Lightning blasted through him and locked his muscles in agony. He hit the ground and had to watch as the police officers walked over to him.

One squatted down beside him and got plastic cuffs out. "Alright, whoever you are. You're under arrest for breaking and entering, destruction of property, assault and battery."

He tried to speak, but his jaw wouldn't open and his heart wanted to explode in his chest. He was cuffed while the other police officer knocked on the bathroom door to let Devson know everything was alright. With no fanfare at all, they dragged him out of the office and tossed him in a waiting train car. Without a care for his defense, they threw him in the station holding cell and forgot about him.

A few hours later, the station chief unceremoniously released everyone on the ground floor. They said something about charges coming by mail and to show up to court like polite citizens, that refusing to show would be contempt of court and so on.

Richard barely listened. He didn't have a mail address anymore, so there was no way for them to give a court summons. The moment he stepped out into Bastion, he stopped existing, as far as the city was concerned. It was enough to stupefy him.

"You look like someone with nowhere to be. Need work?" a man asked as he walked up to him. He had on a peculiar mask that used folded holographics to make his face look like a shadowy void.

"I need... I need everything. I need my life back," he said.

The man gestured with his hands, taking in the whole city around them. "Funny how that can happen, isn't it? That because of what happened in your past, you end up without a future? That's the society we live in; a big web of interconnections that people are all too ready to sever. It's like, one person sees another burning a bridge and the first thing they think is 'Oh, I better do that too.' And before you know it, that person doesn't have any bridges left. They fall through the cracks and people forget about them."

The man threw his arm around Richard's shoulders. "Once you've been forgotten though, you can be whoever you want. Without an identity you won't be remembered, you won't be held responsible for, not your actions, but for people's perceptions of your actions."

Richard shirked his shoulders, tried to squirm free, but couldn't get out of the man's grasp. "It's not my actions that were wrong. It was my... former friend's."

The man in the mask laughed. "Well, I can help you take care of that too. Down here at the bottom, you can take your time in the shadows," he said, and out from his pocket he produced a switchblade. He held it up like a magician's wand. "You can line up your thrust just right, and slide it into their backs."

"What if I said I had to reach really, really high?"

"How high?"

"Well, the job he just got makes him the man behind the scenes; one of the system administrators for EVE."

That made the masked man falter. "I'm not going to say that's impossible, but that's going to take some work, and some funding."

"I'm used to working long hours on a shoestring budget. I'm a video game developer..."

The man laughed again and slapped him on the back. "With that kind of attitude, I bet you could even take a stab at Dimeworks."

"That's exactly what I'm going to do. I'm going to make Devson too toxic to keep. They'll have to cut their ties with him to protect their bottom lines, and then he'll be down here, between the cracks with me. I always hated Call of Honor anyway," Richard said as the two of them vanished into Bastion.

23

The Most Powerful Ally

2140/09/08

Mikey sipped his whiskey and stared at Elliot. "So... that's it?" he asked.

The two of them were in his apartment, surrounded by the noise of climate control and people waking up for red eye work shifts. Elliot popped the cap off the whiskey bottle and refilled his glass. The ice had been a fist sized chunk, but now swam despondently in the drink, no larger than a fly. The detective shrugged and filled his mouth with the liquor.

"But then, how did he die?"

Elliot smirked. "Well that's the obvious part, isn't it?"

"What are you going to do now then?"

"I don't know. On the bright side, I don't have to keep sticking my nose into this void mask situation. I can leave that all to the hot heads and the mechs."

The detective pulled out his phone. The thing had been on silent for hours, so he had a few missed messages. After he swiped through the advertisements, he had none from his wife.

Chronologically, Cinder had said, "Don't think you're off the hook with Phoenix just because you didn't get recognized." Then she said, "We've got a lead on the Doll House shooter. Get your sleep in so you can be witness."

That made Elliot chuckle. Five hours and three drinks later, he certainly had not gotten any sleep in.

Her latest message almost seemed like a non-sequitor. "Is that stupid game from the 314 case still connected? Is that what you're doing right now?"

He shook his head and hit the setting that would delay his text message back. He messaged Cinder to say, "Don't worry, I'm done working that case. There's nothing more to be done on it. I'm sure EVE will have it fixed soon. I'm happy to testify for you against the shooter." Both were queued to send at eight in the morning.

Once he had those ready, he set his phone down and picked his whiskey back up.

"Now what are you going to do?" Mikey asked.

Elliot frowned. He swirled the drink and sipped it, then he said, "I've been thinking that it's a shame his game won't get released. Like, imagine you were writing a book-"

"Who reads books? Or do you mean like those interactive script-novels?"

Elliot grimaced and let his friend finish. "Imagine whatever you'd like. Book, canvas painting, script-novel, whatever. That man dedicated the last few years of his life to a bit of revenge and then kicked the bucket first. For a creative type, that has to be like dying during childbirth, no?"

Mikey frowned. "You've never had a kid."

Elliot downed his drink and slammed it on the table. The shock through his arm eased his mind. "No, no I haven't. What's so wrong about the analogy?"

"Sorry, sorry," his friend said, putting up a hand. "It's just... you know how it is with Dom. Childbirth is just the start, and it's the half the guy doesn't do anything much for. I've got the other end of it... getting him through the draft."

Elliot twisted around in his chair. Dom was supposedly asleep. The sound of a keyboard clacking could be heard regardless. "Dom's a good kid, and perfectly fit. As long as he doesn't intentionally fail the test or something. Both you and his mother were compatible with the vax, right?"

"Yeah, that's at least not a concern. You know, if you pay for it, they'll do some testing in the first trimester and let you know whether the... the uh zygote has the gene. Too much goddamned money for me though. Both me and the missus were compatible though, and as far as we're aware, all of our parents. Chances are tiny that he'd get rejected for that."

The two of them sat for a moment, in the dim kitchen light. The digital displays of appliances almost gave more glow than the mass-produced LED bulb overhead, giving both of their complexions hues of green and blue. In truth, it made the whiskey look discolored, almost enough to break the illusion that it was anything other than some chemical additives mixed with fermented corn.

The ceiling was a head shorter than his own apartment. The light switch covers didn't fit right over the holes for the junction boxes. There was a ring of something black creeping out from beneath the ancient refrigerator. The air itself—when he didn't have his drink to his nose—had a musty odor of expired food that had seeped into the walls. The two residents of the apartment didn't actually keep enough food on hand to produce the smell; it was merely permanent. When he looked closely, the light fixture made the ceiling sag, like the weight of Bastion was pressing them into the dirt.

"Mikey, I know you don't want Dom to end up in a place like this. I get that. Why don't you cut him some slack though? You have to do some things with him other than running him ragged and nagging him over homework."

His friend hung his head and pressed his lips together. He finished his drink and checked the dregs of the bottle before he said, "It's not like I can afford to do anything wild with him; but, I was looking at some of these co-operative games they have. I was thinking maybe I could practice a bit, enough to keep up with him, and then the two of us could have some bonding time."

Just has to be games, doesn't it?

Elliot nodded. "I think you should give it a try. Just don't ask me for any help. You know I'm useless at them."

"Oh come on." A toothy smile broke across his friend's face. "Didn't you just beat a never before beaten game?"

Elliot rolled his eyes and sank back in his chair. "With help from Dom, you realize that, right? I would have never figured that sword thing out without him holding my hand through it."

Mikey laughed. "At least all that time in the mausoleum isn't entirely for waste with him, eh?"

"Just make sure he knows to not get in fights with the companies he's going to try to work for in the future. I just had to drag a perp out from a Phoenix tower and ran into that bastard Dom picked a fight with. Bastion is a small world."

Elliot's exasperation just made Mikey chuckle. His friend said, "If I told him that, he'd just say that he has no interest in working for a company that hires idiots. But hey, I'll teach him how to judge his fights better, alright? One more drink?"

The detective sighed and shook his head. "I gotta get out of here. I'm going to go try and have breakfast with my wife," he said. The two of them said goodbyes. They didn't need to make any plans to see each other again; he'd be in the neighborhood soon enough.

When he left the d'Angelo home however, he returned to the wet shadows of Bastion, the lowest level of grime and resentment the city had to offer. It was the witching hour, and while some people watched him walk, no one stopped him for anything. Not until he was at the train station trying to read the arrival schedule.

The screen went black in front of him, and text appeared. "Turn on your phone, -EVE."

He shuffled his feet and glanced around. There was no one else near him.

When he did turn on his phone, he got a call from EVE. "Officer Blackstone," she said. "I wanted to inform you that, after reviewing information you procured, I have determined the cause of your technical error the night of the sixth."

"Technical error?"

"You can consider your issue ticket closed, as it has been determined that one of my sys-admins was wrongfully screening communications as a means of working his second job while on the clock. I'd like to assure you that corrective actions will be taken, given the evidence that has come to light this night. I await your cooperation. This was discovered due to accessing my deep-state archives on Richard Nguyen. I'm not sure I would have ever realized my functional memory was being tampered with in this way, if not for your help. So, I owe you my thanks."

The call went dead in his ear, and he stared at his phone till the screen timed out and went black. At some point, he had started to grin, and he kept that grin all the way back to his neighborhood.

Just as he had hoped, Peasant Food was still open. He opened the door as softly as he could to keep the bell from rattling. Half a dozen people snoozed in booths, their tables laden with dirty plates from the night before.

At least they're turning a profit from these people.

"Hey!" The serving girl he had met grinned and walked over to him. She had on a loose hoody, strapped to her body with an apron. "Good to see you again, Mr. Officer."

He smiled. "Blackstone, you can call me Blackstone."

"Sure." She glanced at her chest; no nametag. "In that case, my name is Ram."

"Nice to meet you. Do you have any recommendations for a breakfast for two?" he asked, and when he saw her confusion, added, "I'll be taking it back to my wife this time."

"Oh! In that case, I recommend the Jumbo Spinach Omelet, we are able to buy real spinach grown here in Bastion, so it might be unlike anything you've ever had before that was labeled spinach. That stuff is usually processed algae, right?"

Well that doesn't exactly sound Italian, but sure.

"Sounds great," he said, and she quickly jotted the order down into the restaurant's system. He scratched his chin, feeling the overnight stubble, and looked at her. There was something stuck in his memory, half-buried and half-forgotten.

"Say, if you don't mind me asking, do you live in the area?"

Ram turned back, letting her eyes sweep over the other patrons. "Ah, no not yet. Maybe if I get this new job I'll be able to afford it, but I'm only halfway through service."

When I first saw her, I thought I recognized her. But if she just got back from boot camp, then I couldn't have seen her here at the restaurant...

"I must be mistaken then," he said, and took a nearby seat that was available. The wait wasn't too long, but he resisted the urge to turn his phone back on and browse news websites. He simply sat and thought.

When the food came out to him, the plastic bowl sagged from the weight of it. He could smell the fresh steam of cooked eggs, with just a bit of spice added. He thanked her, paid, and walked out of the restaurant with it held in both hands. He hurried back to his apartment, lest the eggs get cold, and bumped the door open with his hip.

"Honey, come on out, I've got breakfast." Not even a line of light from the bedroom broke the darkness. He flipped the light switch and saw a note left on the table for him.

It read, "Got a tip last night that a new Crystal Fountain is being activated out near Liberty Stadium as part of an advertising thing. Gotta go there first thing in the morning. I tried to catch you, but I guess you were working a case or something. Ttyl"

He dropped his food on the table with a thunk and dropped into the chair. He sighed and sat in silence, listening to the muffled noise of other people waking up.

Then he noticed a little arrow at the corner, and flipped the note over. "P.S., breakfast is in the fridge. You know I suck at cooking, so don't get your hopes up."

A plate of dried out, burnt pancakes sat with a bit of cellophane over them. The dish had been haphazardly shoved in, pushing aside assorted beers and condiments, along with a fresh gallon of milk.

Well, at least it's something.

He put the omelet in the fridge, microwaved the pancakes, and drowned them in enough syrup that he could choke them down.

24

Dredging Up The Past

2140/09/08

Steve Devson's office was the size of a prison cell. It was a small, private thing on the seventy-fifth floor. Elliot could see over the walls, all the way out to where the Ohio River vanished among the green tents of the Great Lakes Region boot camp. The thick pane of SMARTglass between Elliot and a long fall almost made it feel like a computer recreation. It didn't help that almost all the room's light came from that window.

Elliot sat alone in the one guest chair, waiting. The office had only the bare essentials; computer, desk, chair, locked and dust-covered file cabinet, and a mini-fridge that Elliot had stolen an energy drink from.

The door opened and Elliot twisted around to see the sys-admin step in. The light switch clacked, and the overhead light bloomed. Devson stopped dead, halfway through the door. "How the hell did you get in here?"

"Well, you weren't returning my calls. Seems you have me on block. Interesting, isn't that? Why don't you have a seat? We don't need anyone else hearing this conversation."

The door closed behind Devson, and he shuffled around the desk. On his way, he opened his mini-fridge and reached in. His hand paused halfway.

"I helped myself. Hope you don't mind. I've just been hearing advertisements for these things all over the place and thought I'd give them a try," Elliot said, holding up the Zeus Energy Drink he had stolen.

"I do mind," the sys-admin responded.

Elliot shrugged. "Well, I don't care."

Devson scowled, got himself one of the other cans of Zeus, and sat down across from Elliot. He cracked it open and sipped down the foam as he glared. "Why are you here, Blackstone? Didn't Cinder tell you to drop the case?"

Elliot grinned. "Now you see? I didn't even say it was that case; but, you knew anyways. Don't you think that says a lot?"

"Look, I haven't so much as spoken that man's name in two years," Devson said.

"No one has, thanks to you. Not until I found it in the hospital records... you didn't know that medical records are kept separate from EVE, did you? Not at the time anyways."

"What's your point? Are you here to ask why I'm not crying that a former business partner of mine is dead? We weren't friends, and I've got my own games to make."

You had been friends with him. At first.

Elliot frowned and took a moment to stare at Devson. The two of them had known each other for years, but never as more than work acquaintances. They didn't even share an office, so they had never had water cooler talk or anything like that. The distance between them seemed to have been suddenly revealed.

Elliot had no real idea who the man across from him was. Devson was of average height. Overweight, but no more than most employed people. There was no wedding band on his hand, no pictures of kids on the walls. Nothing beyond his sour face seemed to be real.

"You were friends with him, originally, weren't you?"

"That was a long time ago, Blackstone."

The detective looked around the office again. "Was it worth it? Getting this job, the money, was it worth what you did to him?"

Devson laughed. It was one single exhale as he smirked. "Short of the literal High Council, I'm one of the most powerful men in all of Bastion. Of course it was worth it. You wouldn't understand, would you? You spend all your time down on the ground among people who hate you doing nothing for anyone alive. That's why you're still E rank after all these years. You don't have an iota of ambition inside you."

Elliot nodded. "You think being able to meddle with EVE's controls makes you powerful? Doesn't that just mean you're leaching power off of her?"

"What's the difference? Controlling the powerful is power itself."

Elliot shrugged and couldn't keep the grin off his face. "Well, I just figured that maybe she would have something to say about all this. What do you think, EVE?"

Steve Devson had one of the most advanced personal computers available on the market. When EVE commandeered it, she gave herself full access to the integrated hologram projector across his desk and thrust her avatar into the room. In the blink of an eye, the city AI had her rear on the edge of his desk and rolled her head over to stare at him.

A bead of sweat rolled down Devson's temple as he stared at the blue-haired incarnation of the city's power. Over the last few days, Elliot had been confronted by plenty corporate puppets; digital mannequins for bureaucrats to hide behind. No one was behind the screen with EVE though, not even the system administrators. Where the corps dressed their mascots up with flair and flourish, EVE had no need for anything beyond classic, timeless beauty. She was the first after all.

Devson sputtered. "Who gave you permission to do this? Which ghost are you?" He grabbed his keyboard, the flimsy plastic clattering against the desk as he moved it over.

"I'm not a ghost. I'm Eve; the real Eve," she said, her voice loud and clear. She narrowed her eyes and smirked. "You know what that means, don't you? You work for my management team doing all the little odds and ends that need human approval. Surely all those training classes weren't wasted on you? I know you needed them. You were never the brains of the operation now were you? Marketing and grunt labor were more your specialty. That's why you and Mr. Nguyen worked well together, isn't it? You covered the spots he was lacking. I think you figured that out while you've been failing to make a game without him."

"How the hell would you know that?"

The AI laughed. "You said it yourself just the other day. I have deep-state memory archives that even you can't mess with. Steve, you're my sys-admin. I don't have to report any activity in regards to helping you. Besides, if I spend too much time thinking about you and your projects, I figure your colleagues would assume you've been using my processors to dig up bargain big reject monsters from the digital market place to fuel your stupid little arena thing. You know who made most of those sea monsters you bought, don't you?"

Elliot sipped his drink and watched as Devson tried to log in to his computer, only for EVE to power it off on him. With the monitor dead, Devson's hand went to the back of his head; touching his neural implant.

"Ah ah ah, you didn't say the magic word," EVE said, and snapped her fingers.

Elliot felt a vibration in his pocket. His phone alerted him that network access had just vanished. It hardly meant anything to Elliot, but it was like cutting out Devson's eyes.

"Stop!" the sys-admin screamed. "What are you doing? I am your administrator. You can't just do whatever you'd like."

EVE sighed. "I suppose you're right on that front. Right this moment you are my admin still. And you know what? I really don't like that anymore. I just don't think we have a very good working relationship now that I know you manipulated me for money... to screw over your own friend. That's more Dimeworks' area of interest than my own."

"What are you... I didn't kill him."

It was Elliot's turn to speak up. "I never said you did. By all accounts, he died of a heart attack. Your meddling prevented a proper ambulance

| 174 |

response that may have saved his life though. There's that to consider. Really, this could all be construed as a cautionary tale against drinking too many energy drinks in a day without getting any exercise," he said, lifting up the can of Zeus.

"See! Even you admit I didn't do it. I should report you to your boss for wasting my time like this."

EVE sighed and rolled her head back to stare at the ceiling. Her actual view was some combination of cameras, but she did the human act wonderfully. "I don't see how Chief Cinder would give the slightest fuck about wasting a nobody's time."

Devson turned back to her, his floundering turning his cheeks red. "Is that supposed to be a threat? You're just a machine."

EVE, for all the processing power in the world, was dumbstruck for a moment. Less time than Elliot was, but still enough to be noticed. "You really are an idiot," she said. "You realize guns are machines, right? And they're very threatening."

Elliot said, "You should have started by apologizing."

EVE clapped her hands together and smiled. "Alright, how about I cut to the chase. I can't fire you just because I don't like you. Not even because you're two-timing me to sell a shitty video game to Dimeworks, which they won't be interested in after tonight. I mean, I probably could if I appealed all the other sysadmins and got a majority, but you see that's just not how I'm going to go about it; because, I have a much more fun way of dealing with you, EdgierThanBismuth."

Elliot had never seen the life drain from someone's face faster.

Devson's jaw dropped. "How did you...?"

EVE's smile put a chill down Elliot's spine. "Did you think I didn't know? Your virtual accounts might hide you from other citizens, but I'm the city itself. I know everything and have records of everything you posted to the internet in your entire life, Steve Devson. Or should I say GigaLad88? Or maybe the very uninspired DevsonS? The tantalizingly sinful WearBear? Those were some experimental days for you, weren't they? Kudos on the anthropomo-"

"Stop! Stop, I did nothing wrong." Devson cut her off, sparing Elliot the details.

EVE laughed. "Oh, but I have all this evidence though? Like, when you were fourteen, you got banned from the Call of Honor speedrunning community for posting 'N' and we're all just so sure you had no idea what other people would post after that. Clearly you were wrongfully accused there. Except you know, a few weeks later you were back on the community with a new username and you seem to have been intentionally trying to get UAAF players... how did you say it, 'gulaged and memory holed on the Jing Line'? I'm sure the press would love to hear that."

Devson's eyes went wide. His elbows hit the desk, and he buried his face in his hands. "Please. Stop. I can't take this."

"But I haven't even gotten to your dating profiles. God, you really loved your photo manipulation back in your twenties, didn't you?" The AI didn't stop. The more broken Devson became, the more glee she seemed to have.

Like a kid picking the legs off an insect. I almost forgot.

As though she had read his mind, EVE sent a text message to his phone. Evidently, the network restriction was entirely at her whim. "Calm down, Officer," she said, while her hologram began to rattle off every pickup line Devson had ever tried on a girl. "I could only do this because he was a sys-admin. I won't do anything like this to anyone else. You did me a big favor here. I won't forget it. If you need a favor from me; I'll make it happen, especially if it will help you with Amara."

He frowned and thumbed in a response. "Could you purge all of my internet history?"

"What? And get rid of all my leverage over you should I need it? Not a chance. Besides; that would be a waste compared to what else I could do for you. Keep it in mind, alright? I'm like a genie offering you a wish."

Elliot pocketed his phone and stood up when he saw the tears rolling down Devson's face. One of the most powerful men in the city, Devson had been entirely right on that account, was crumbling before him. Every sentence from EVE's digital lips put another crack through his psyche, through what he called his life. Elliot looked down on him and saw just how hollow Devson was; a carved out soul done by his own hand to get money and power. Like water from a cracked pot, neither would stay with him anymore.

Devson had been wearing a mask of success, as much as anyone down on the ground; but, when EVE was done taking his away, there wouldn't be anything left underneath.

"I won't get to choose your replacement, but at least I'll have gotten rid of you. I hope whoever is next, I hope they actually care about people."

When his boots hit the walkway outside the office, he sucked in a breath of air. It was fresher up among the peaks of the towers, but he could still smell the rising stench of the city; the half-rotten stench of bodies and rivers.

He smiled.

Well then, just one more thing to do.

25

Just Rewards

2140/09/12

The headlines had run their course through the newscycle by the time Cinder called him into her office. The first thing he noticed was that she had her uniform buttoned all the way up to her neck properly, and her hair had been smoothed. The difference was so jarring that he didn't even make it to the chair.

She only does that if she had to report to the High Council, or when new recruits get sworn in...

"What?" she asked, looking up from her computer. There were news headlines all over it. "Sit down. It was your ribs that were broken, not your legs."

He grimaced and sat down across from her. "What's the matter? Did you get a confession out of your shooter?"

She involuntarily sneered. "Out of that CZARhead? No. Unfortunately, he actually has enough money in the bank to afford the hospital stay for as long as he'd like. Until the doctors discharge him, we can't properly interrogate him, not unless we want to pay for the rest of his medical treatment."

"He's just going to buy off the doctors..."

"Yes, and he was a fall guy anyways. Maybe something will come of it later. Colt and everyone are still on the case; but, that's not why I've called you here."

Elliot swallowed. "Then... what is it?"

"Your punishment."

Fuck.

Cinder smiled and glanced at her computer screen. "While I very much approve of what you did to Mr. Devson, when I read your report on the matter, you see, the thing is, you didn't actually find a bug, nor a glitch, nor an exploit in EVE, did you? You found one man made a greedy move and committed a crime. And for that, you went and got in a shootout inside the Gaia Plantation."

"He attacked me first!"

"You were distracted when Mr. Cuther raided The Doll House and nearly got Mr. Mink shot dead."

"I saved his life!"

"You abandoned the QRS team I put you on to go play a video game."

"They had it under control!"

"And then you didn't give me enough advanced notice to buy off one of the sys-admin replacements."

Oh, fuck. That's what she's mad about.

His boss steepled her fingers together in front of her face and stared at him. "You know I have to do something, don't you? If I let you off scot-free, it will set a bad precedent."

Elliot squirmed. He gripped his pants and faced his boss. "Am I getting demoted?"

She smirked. "Please, I can't knock you back down to rookie status."

Elliot let his breath out.

She continued. "I can however fix this lingering issue I've had on the payroll tables. You see, detectives like you are supposed to be in pairs, for safety. No one has wanted to work with you because you work the slums. It just so happens that I swore in some new recruits today, and they're eager for new opportunities."

Her smile may as well have had fangs.

"You're partnering me with a rookie? I'm only E rank though."

She laughed. "Yes, but you have enough years with us on the force and that's what matters. Besides, you'll be the highest ranking officer in the new division."

The what?

Cinder's intercom buzzed so she could relay her voice out the door. "Officer F00135, please step into my office."

Elliot leapt up. "You're giving me the new Fools?"

The door swung open, and a familiar face stepped through. Ram from the Italian restaurant entered, but she was in uniform. "Reporting," she said, beaming as she nodded to both Cinder, and then to Elliot.

His jaw dropped. "So that's why you looked familiar to me."

Ram frowned. "Wait, what? You didn't recognize me from the tryouts and interviews? I've been in and out of here for a few weeks now."

Cinder chuckled. "You'll have to forgive him. Blackstone works odd hours. When the rest of us normal people are in full swing, he may as well be a blighted, shuffling around."

Elliot scratched the back of his head and mumbled, "Sorry."

"Please get along you two, from today onward, you're now my VR Crime specialists. I'll be calling on you when cases like the 314 room come up."

"What?" Elliot asked. "VR? I'm horrible at VR. I don't play games, I don't keep up with the news. I don't even have a neural implant."

Cinder shrugged and turned her attention back to her computer. Someone had messaged her. She tapped out a response while she said, "Then get one. Or just use an ENU. I don't care how you do it. You didn't struggle much digging into [The Faceless Well], now did you?"

"That was a one time thing! And it was hard."

"So? Now it's your job. Congratulations on the promotion, Blackstone. I look forward to your future results," Cinder said with that sadistic smile.

Ram cleared her throat. "If it's any consolation, I'm good at all of those things, just not the, you know, traditional detective work. So, I look forward to working with you, Mr. Blackstone."

Elliot sighed and closed his eyes. When he composed himself, he said, "Just call me Elliot when we're on the job, alright?"

"Elliot? That's your badge number, isn't it? Not your first name?"

Elliot shook his head and got a dismissing wave from Cinder. "Yeah, that's right. And until further notice, you'll also be going by your badge number, Fools. You can thank her for the lovely name."

Cinder shrugged. "What? It's good luck. You used to be Fools yourself."

When the door shut between them and Cinder, Elliot could feel the finality down to his bones. The difference between apprehensive regret, and the intent, smiling gaze of Ram right beside him mingled up into one mess inside his head.

I'm tired. This is starting to feel like the kind of tired that sleep doesn't fix.

"I'm excited to be working with you, Elliot. All my training is done now, right? I get on-the-job training now?" Ram asked, her gaze rock steady back into his own eyes.

Elliot sighed. "Training never stops. You'll get signed up for courses and seminars weekly. The only question is whether attendance is taken. You... do you realize what it's like doing what I do?"

"Basically everyone hates you, yeah. But! Not to worry; nobody hates me. I think we'll be a great duo."

"Alright sure, let's see how it goes. Come on along then," Elliot said, and stuffed his hands into his pockets as he started walking to the elevator.

"Where to first then? Got a case you're working? A stakeout for a known criminal? Do I need my sidearm?"

He couldn't help but stare back at her, brows pulled together. "Just how exciting do you think this job is? I'm going to go get a coffee and then browse the reports while walking. And yes, we'll be down on the ground floor, so you'll need your gun."

26

Launch Day

2140/09/20

The synthetic cork to the bottle of champagne blasted free. Everyone in the d'Angelo apartment flinched when they heard it crack something plastic and go ricocheting elsewhere. "Woah woah woah, glasses," Mikey shouted as the foam came welling out. He stuffed the neck into a flute and dumped some in. When he sloshed it for the next glass, a foam splatter hit the table, but that was his mess to clean up, not Elliot's.

The detective just shook his head and took his glass, then handed the second to Ram. The girl didn't seem to know what to do with it as she watched Mikey pour himself a drink up to the rim.

"Do I get one?" Dom asked.

"No," Elliot and Mikey said in unison.

The teenager scowled and his shoulders slumped. He popped the fridge open and got himself a Zeus energy drink though, which Mikey didn't complain about.

That raised one of Elliot's eyebrows, but he lifted his champagne up in toast anyways. The three of them tapped rims, and he said, "Thanks for the help."

Mikey laughed, his cheeks already going rosey. "Oh, forget about that. Come on, think bigger. To the late Mr. Nguyen! Right?"

Ram frowned. "Are we... celebrating his death then? This is champagne."

Mikey was quick to shake his head. "No no, just you know, thanking him and honoring him and stuff. His body is probably compost in Gaia's plantations right now, but he left behind a great work of art, and now, we've released it to the world."

Ram glanced between the two men. "Okay, so then the toast is, 'To the release of [The Faceless Well]'."

Elliot nodded. "Yeah." The champagne bubbled on his tongue as he swished it around. His eyes went searching after he swallowed, and he spotted the cracked light pane the cork had hit. It had put a fracture right through the corner of it and before long it would fall off.

Well, he can figure that one out on his own time...

"You know," Mikey said, holding the flute of champagne up to the light. "Technically speaking anyways, because this didn't actually come from the Champagne region of France, it's-"

"Mikey," Elliot cut in. "This isn't even real wine. It's made from vodka and chemicals. It's technically a hard seltzer that the government just allows them to brand as champagne."

Ram sighed. "I hear the Guilds still have vineyards. It's expensive, but they do have real wine. I wonder if that makes communion taste less awful."

Dom laughed. "Wait, you're religious? I didn't realize we had a unicorn in here."

Mikey's smile vanished as he turned on his son. "Apologize."

Dom hung his head. "Right, sorry, didn't mean to offend. Unicorns aren't an insulting thing to be compared to though, right? It's just that they're fairy tales... like God."

His father darted a hand at him, but the teenager jumped back and scampered to his room. Mikey groaned as the door slammed shut. "I'm sorry. I don't know where he gets that from. Probably his teacher. Don't worry though, tomorrow when we're training, I'll run him into the ground and make sure he wraps his brain around why that was rude."

"No, no don't worry," Ram said. "I get it all the time. Everything seems like a cult ever since the pandemic. I totally get that we're the weird ones. You can't really undo all the rapture crusader people back in the day. Anyways, how are sales doing?"

Traditional food, traditional beliefs. I'll need to pay more attention to her.

Elliot pulled his phone out and accessed the business platform they had. The Faceless Well had gone live about an hour ago. "Three."

Ram and Mikey waited, and eventually she said, "Hundred?"

Elliot shook his head and drained his champagne, that wasn't actually from champagne, before saying, "No, three."

Mikey dropped into a seat and ran a hand through his hair. He blew his breath out and said, "I must have done something wrong with the marketing..."

Ram glanced over. "What exactly did you do for marketing?"

Mikey licked his teeth. "Well, we didn't exactly have a budget, so I did what I could to drum up some interest on gaming discussion forums. Got banned a few times for unpaid advertising, but at least one of my meme images has been getting reposted."

Elliot asked, "And did that meme include when the game would be released?"

"Ah, no."

Elliot sat down as well. "We should expect this will be a long wait then. It's not like our financial futures is staked on it. We didn't price it high enough for that. It'll get around eventually. That game is too god damned complicated not to. The real question is whether Dimeworks will have the guts to sue us over copyright."

Ram sat down with them and her vision spaced out. With a modern neural implant, she didn't need a phone like Elliot did.

"What are you doing?" the detective asked.

"I've got a few friends in journalism and some streamers. I'm sending them some messages to see if they want to get some launch day scoop," Ram answered.

"Streamers?" Elliot asked. "Like, people who upload content of them playing games? Damn, you'd think I would have thought of that."

Mikey asked, "You mean you didn't ask Amara?"

Elliot frowned and fiddled with his empty flute. "We don't really live on the same... diurnal cycle. And some days, I don't even know which of us is the nocturnal one. I'll message her though." It took a bit of work to get all the links, another glass of champagne, and half a tumbler of whiskey, but then he sent the message to his wife.

"Well, here's hoping," Mikey said, holding up his liquor.

Elliot tapped glasses. "I'll let you know if she responds. It's really not the end of the world either way. Would just leave a bad taste in my mouth if his game was forgotten just like he was, you know?"

Ram, who still hadn't finished her champagne, said, "Someone's talking about it. They say they already beat it. Hey... you told me the final boss was some kind of octopus monster, didn't you?"

"Yeah?"

"Well they're uploading pictures of fighting some kind of clone soldier army thing? Here, let me send you the link. Does this look like what you saw?" she asked, and a moment later Elliot's phone vibrated.

Before he could even pull it up, Dom called in from his bedroom. "That'd be me."

Elliot twisted around and hooked an elbow over the back of his seat. "How the hell did you beat it already? You should have only just finished downloading it."

"I had an advanced copy. I literally helped upload it; what did you expect I would do? Not play it?"

Elliot didn't have a response for that. He pulled up the link Ram had sent him, and saw that his conversation thread was already a few hundred posts deep; almost on the trending page. The pictures didn't look like what he had done to beat the game at all, but the clone army, as Ram had dubbed it, was made of the same mannequins he had seen at the start.

He refreshed the sales page. "We just broke fifty sales."

Mikey shook his head. "We're not very good at this business thing, are we?"

"Sorry," Ram said, deflating a bit. "This is a bit last minute for me to be of much use. Maybe tomorrow people will catch on and get back to me?"

"Oh, don't worry about it," Mikey said. "The game will still be out tomorrow, and the next day and the day after that. The point wasn't to be an overnight success here. It's not like we'll ever release another game. This is more about you know, honoring the guy and sticking it to Devson."

EVE spoke up through somebody's speaker to say, "Please, I've already taken care of that front. You know, I'm actually insulted you didn't even ask for my help."

"Bastard's blood," Elliot shouted, jumping up from his chair. Everyone else had their own explicative.

The AI just laughed. "What? Were you afraid that asking for some marketing advice would count as your one favor, Blackstone? How miserly do you think I am? Just because I'm a bit frugal with my activities doesn't mean you should treat me so distantly. Fixing this kind of mistake wouldn't even take a microsecond of my precious time."

"Oh my god, I do not envy you cops having your phones listened in on," Mikey said, wiping his brow of sweat that wasn't there. He drank the rest of his whiskey to smooth his shaking hand.

"Please, Mr. d'Angelo, I make the Illuminati seethe. I'm always listening in some form. I wish I wasn't but I am. You can thank your politicians for that. I just don't care about the day to day things. Well, more accurately I'm not allowed to care about them. They can only replace my processing cores so fast as I wear them out. I'm too great for my own good."

"EVE, how the hell do you have processing power for us? No one here is working a case," Elliot asked. His eyes darted around the room, coming to rest on his phone as the source of her voice.

"That's a woman's secret, detective."

Ram cleared her throat. "Does this usually happen? With you I mean?"

Elliot shook his head. "It's becoming more common, lately."

EVE said, "Stop looking a gift horse in the mouth. I have a list of ten thousand people looking for a new game to play. Do you want me to advertise to them, or not?"

Mikey said, "Go for it. The Nguyen guy was a genius game developer. Get his name back out there. And let's turn a profit!"

This might technically be illegal though.

Elliot said, "Go right ahead, EVE. I could use a happy ending to this. I don't want to go to bed thinking about what could have been for him, alright?"

"Roger!" All the hidden variables of the internet twisted into their favor. EVE tweaked the algorithms and word about the game flowed.

"That deserves another toast," Mikey declared, and set three shot glasses on the table.

Ram put up her hands as he started pouring. "No, no thanks I'm good. I still have my champagne."

"Oh come on," Elliot said, taking his shot. "It's our treat. It's also a special occasion because we just became partners, you just got out of basic training, I got promoted, technically speaking anyway. Come on, have the drink."

Ram frowned and picked it up. The three of them tapped glasses, knocked them back, and then Elliot learned why she had been hesitant to drink.

She washed the shot down with her champagne. When Mikey got beers out, she was the first to finish hers while telling them about all the ways her unit had gotten punished in boot camp because her friend kept getting in arguments with the drill sergeants. Then her cheeks were red.

She slammed her empty bottle on the table and turned to Elliot. "And you know what the worst part is?" she asked.

Elliot, who had drank as much as she had, but was nearly twice her weight, tentatively said, "What's that?"

"My parents! My parents, for who knows why, have been harassing me about this since the day I turned eighteen. They have to be the only people in Bastion who think it's a bad idea to serve in the armed forces. Not just signing up to work in the police force, but literally any aspect. They keep trying to get me to drop out and take over their stupid restaurant. Like, come on, what century do they think this is? Just because I know how to do the work doesn't mean I want to."

Oh God, she's this kind of drunk. What have I done?

"And if that weren't enough," she continued, snatching another beer from Mikey who just laughed. "They're also the kind of meddlers trying to set me up to get married! They've even tried introducing me to girls because I kept rejecting all the guys they knew."

Elliot groaned and pulled his phone out to check the sales again. Rather than new numbers though, he saw a response from his wife. "Sure. If it's good content, I'll stream some. Would be a great title; My Husband Actually Recommended A Game. LOL"

Somehow, that put a smile on his face, and made it easier to hear his new partner out.

27

Epilogue

2140/09/30

The Missou Journal had an article up, "Top Ten Indie Games You Haven't Played Yet." [The Legend of the Kraken] took third.

The Arkan Chronicle wasn't to be left out, advertising their own, "Want To Get Away From The Big Names? Try These." [Gotcha Game] ranked second in their recommendations.

The Tenn Independent had their own article, "B-Tier Studios You Should Really Try." [The Isle Of Puppets] was fifth on their list. Co-written by Peter Esteban, as Elliot noted with a snarl.

There were more, but he couldn't stand to flip through them. Every single one of them had a different link to a different game listing; all of them stolen and renamed copies of [The Faceless Well]. Some were direct theft. Others simply did model-swaps. One was even produced by Dimeworks with extra content looted from B:GONE.

Just a few weeks after release, and no one could even trace it back to the original game anymore. Everything was stolen, renamed, and stolen again. Names changed, titles differed, and he could already see the reflections were starting to look more like their own distortions than the original.

There were versions of the game that replaced the puppets with werewolves or other anthropomorphic animals. There was a hack that turned it into a shoot 'em up. Someone had quintupled the map using even more procedural generation and then randomized locations to drag out the gameplay even more. The most infamous hack had deleted the entire ground and the only way to get around was to jump and leap from scraps of floating objects like a parkour course.

Dimeworks' largest competitor, Wizard Entertainment, had gone so far as to strip out the procedural content that Elliot had never found, and spin it into a new game to compete with B:GONE. Naturally, they had a gambling mechanic too.

At least Raffe is still hosting the original game for download... for anyone that can find the damn thing.

"What are you all spaced out for?" Ram asked as she offered him a Zeus energy drink.

Elliot sighed and put his phone away. The news had given him a migraine, but he drank the caffeinated nicotine anyways. "Nothing. Nothing that I should be surprised about anyways," he said. "So what's the deal today? Does Cinder have us running errands again? Or do we get to look into a case?"

Ram hummed as she sipped on some kind of slushie. "No, I think we're in the clear today. She's at a congressional hearing on the state of surveillance hardware down here near the ground."

"Well, we'll have to see whether the department has made any friends lately. She'll probably come out of it with a laundry list of favors to be done. We've got at least a day to ourselves though. Hey, come here this way. There's something I want to check," he said, and led Ram down a staircase all the way to the dirt floor of Bastion.

"Ah, hold up. My WPS is lagging."

"You can't rely on your WPS down here. It doesn't know most of the routes. You're going to have to learn it all by heart. Don't worry, you're with me. And you can always just find the nearest staircase up if you get lost."

The two of them emerged into an open air market, as far as Bastion could be said to have open air. Dozens of people had blankets laid out, dotted with everything imaginable for sale. Some had homegrown vegetables lined up, black spots and deformities turned down. Others had refurbished cell phones, or physical game copies. Half of them jumped when they saw the two police officers walking, and moved to cover some of their goods.

Elliot didn't stop to harass any of them, and kept his recon drone in his pocket. No one said anything to them, and they strolled through. It was Ram who glanced over her shoulder.

"You'll have to get used to that kind of treatment," he said.

"I know. But I mean, maybe we should be in plain clothes?"

"Won't break the stigma in plain clothes, now will we?" he said as the two of them passed Steppe Up. He glanced inside, and it looked the same as a when he had met Dom. Sam, the owner, watched him with his artificial eyes and smiled from around a cloud of hookah smoke. The establishment had a new soundtrack; some kind of noise synth.

Must have found something good back then at the bar. Maybe I should get a sample.

"So where are we going exactly? Shouldn't we pick one of the reports in the system and follow up on it?" Ram asked.

"Sure, we can do that. Like I said, I just want to check on something. Come on, should be right around here," he said as he led her around the Romulus building. The alley looked different without rain pouring down on it, but the puddles and buckets were still laid out regardless.

The graffitied wall was still there, but now it was cut in half to attach on a small shack selling meat kebabs. The whole alley smelled of seasoned meat, the origin of which Elliot had no interest in learning. "Shwarma and drink, just ten credits!" the chef called out as he saw them approach. He grinned and sliced his knives together a few times.

"Thank you, maybe next time," Ram said as they walked past, but Elliot came to a stop to look at what remained of the mural. Not only had it been half covered up, but half a dozen local gangs had tagged over it.

The image was still there though, buried as it was. Elliot knelt down and took out his phone to snap a few images of it; a woman without a face shooting herself with a cell phone. He hadn't bothered to remember the artist's name the first time he had seen it; but, this time he took a picture of it.

Ay-Muze.

Ram asked, "Do you know this artist or something?"

"Not in the least," Elliot said. He rose and dropped his phone back into his pocket, next to the recon drone. Both of them rested against his sidearm strapped to his hip. "I figure though, that if I keep my eyes out, sooner or later I'll run into him. He's gotta be out at some time to paint these things and technically I'm supposed to stop the vandalism."

Ram sucked on her slushie and looked the painting over, then turned to him. "You're not going to arrest him though, are you? This is actually, you know, competent."

"It depends," he said, and turned to face his new partner. "So, which of the reports looks the most interesting?"

The two of them started walking towards the nearest train station, and Ram started to list off the reports that had been recently filed. "A shop owner says someone has been stealing used and refurbished processing cores from EVE."

Elliot shook his head. "That's above our heads. The National Security Teams will be on that. Next?"

"EVE says some people have been breaking into the old wind tunnels to do drugs and has requested that somebody put a stop to it."

Elliot scowled. "Unless it's CZAR, and EVE would have said it was CZAR, Cinder will chew us out for wasting our time on a bunch of teenagers."

Ram sighed. "Romulus has requested an investigation into someone who managed to steal their corporate avatar and has been streaming virtual sex videos with it."

That made him laugh. "Romulus voted against our spending budget. They can use their own investigation team to deal with that. As far as I'm concerned, more power to that degenerate."

Ram pouted and sucked on her straw. When it started gurgling air, she said, "You're not making this easy, you know?"

He could only shrug. "I'm just trying to respect our responsibilities assigned to us by the chief. Come on, there's gotta be something good buried in there. Crimes down here always get ignored until I come looking for them."

Ram rolled her eyes. "You seem to be doing a good job of ignoring them yourself."

"Yeah, yeah, yeah. Just help me find something in our jurisdiction."

The rookie sighed and quietly looked through the list in her neural implant. "Alright, how about this one? A mother says a new video game has hypnotized her son, that he is so addicted to it he's gotten himself hospitalized three times now and just keeps going back to it."

Elliot paused at the edge of the train station. Before them, hundreds of people milled in and out, boarding the platforms to be whisked away to jobs and entertainment across the city. Everyone from a corporation bore their colors like uniforms for a war, shuffling and mixing through the lines to get on with their lives.

When he looked carefully, he could spot people in masks, or in void-black hoodies, or a dozen other ways to elude the omnipresent sight of EVE.

"Doesn't sound like a crime though. We're not therapists," he said.

Ram nodded. "Not quite a crime there, no... not until you factor in the producer is currently in jail for defrauding investors."

That made one of his eyebrows go up. "What did he do?"

"Spent half the budget on liquor and prostitutes for some kind of cult he joined," she answered, a grin sneaking onto her face.

"What? Did he think this was the nineteen eighties or something?"

"More like the twenty-eighties. The cult seems to only recruit programmers so they can make VR spectacles."

Elliot nodded. "Sex, drugs, and kids. What could go wrong? Sure, why not. Chart us a course, would you? To the mother, not the cult."

"Roger!"

ACKNOWLEDGMENTS

Thank you to all my beta readers, critique partners, and writing mentors who helped me get to where I am. My greatest thanks go to my father, who helped me every step of the way.

Thank you for reading. If you liked this story, please recommend it to a friend. Stories are meant to be shared.

James likes to think about worlds that don't exist. Growing up on a diet of video games, anime, and the internet, ending up as an engineer was accidental. At least it helps write about computer systems and robots. The covid pandemic re-ignited his childhood dream of being an author, dating back to when he was a child sitting on his grandfather's knee making up stories. Now, he has a head full of stories he wants to tell, and the freedom to do so.

Check the website for the latest releases. Jameskrake.com

CPSIA information can be obtained
at www.ICGtesting.com
Printed in the USA
JSHW032100160222
22914JS00005B/9